"You're amazingly flexible, Cody,

Liann said. "Just look at all the new things you've done since you've been here."

He tucked a wandering strand of hair behind her ear so he could have an unobstructed view of her profile. "Like what?"

"Well, you've learned a lot about the myths and legends of the islands, you've met a native priest, you've experienced a blessing."

"That's it?" His brows rose in inquiry.

"Isn't it enough?"

"You've forgotten one thing."

"What?"

Cody's hand cupped her bare shoulder, and he looked down at her uplifted face. "Not forgotten, actually. You never knew."

"What?"

"That I want you."

Dear Reader:

The spirit of the Silhouette Romance Homecoming Celebration lives on as each month we bring you six books by continuing stars!

And there are some wonderful stories in the stars for you. During the coming months, we're publishing romances by many of your favorite authors, including Brittany Young, Lucy Gordon and Rita Rainville. In addition, we have some very special treats planned for the fall and winter of 1988.

In October, watch for *Tyler*—Book III of Diana Palmer's exciting trilogy, Long, Tall Texans. Diana's handsome Tyler is sure to lasso your heart—forever!

Also in October is Annette Broadrick's *Come Be My Love*—the exciting sequel to *That's What Friends Are For*. Remember Greg Duncan, the mysterious bridegroom? Well, sparks fly when he meets his match—Brandi Martin!

And Sal Giordiano, the handsome detective featured in *Sherlock's Home* by Sharon De Vita, is returning in November with his own story—*Italian Knights*.

There's plenty more for you to discover in the Silhouette Romance line during the fall and winter. So as the weather turns colder, enjoy the warmth of love while you are reading Silhouette Romances. Your response to these authors and other authors of Silhouette Romances has served as a touchstone for us, and we're pleased to bring you more books with Silhouette's distinctive medley of charm, wit and—above all—*romance*.

I hope you enjoy this book and the many stories to come. Come home to Silhouette Romance—for always!

Sincerely,

Tara Hughes
Senior Editor
Silhouette Books

RITA RAINVILLE

Valley of Rainbows

Published by Silhouette Books New York

America's Publisher of Contemporary Romance

For Jill Landis who shared her island with me,
Gini Wilson for helping me understand the Kahuna
and
Bob and Diana Rodriguez who found the heart of
their dreams in Kona

SILHOUETTE BOOKS
300 E. 42nd St., New York, N.Y. 10017

ISBN: 0-373-08598-2

First Silhouette Books printing September 1988

Printed in the U.S.A.

RITA RAINVILLE

This award-winning writer has been happily married to the same man for twenty-nine years. They live in Southern California near their two sons and custom-made daughter-in-law. She has been a romantic all of her life and never plans to change. Winner of the *Romantic Times* 1987 Love and Laughter award, Rita firmly believes that humor, as well as love, makes the world go round.

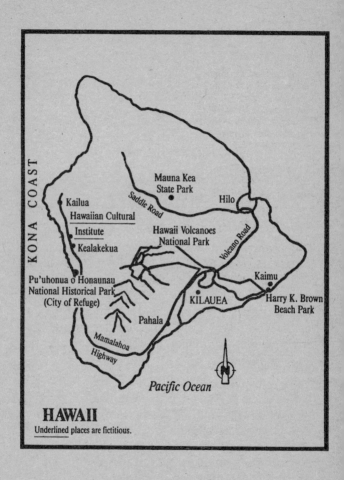

KONA COAST

Mauna Kea
State Park

Saddle Road

Hilo

Kailua
Hawaiian Cultural
Institute

Hawaii Volcanoes
National Park

Volcano Road

Kealakekua

Pu'uhonua o Honaunau
National Historical Park
(City of Refuge)

Kaimu

KILAUEA

Harry K. Brown
Beach Park

Pahala

Mamalahoa
Highway

N

Pacific Ocean

HAWAII
Underlined places are fictitious.

Chapter One

The first week, Liann Murphy gave Cody Hunter the benefit of the doubt. The second week, she stretched it a bit farther. By the third, she had developed a nervous twitch.

It wasn't fair, she thought, that—

Now what?

Alerted by the abrupt silence, Liann's head tilted for a moment as she waited for the resumption of the familiar rumblings. When it didn't come, she slid from her perch on the corner of the large desk and stepped over to the window of the trailer. Looking out over the area enclosed by a chain link fence and dotted with heavy equipment that had been systematically gouging holes in the ground, she zeroed in on the big man standing with his fists jammed on his hips.

He was so blasted stubborn!

He was also gorgeous, she admitted reluctantly. One hundred ninety pounds of solid muscle and bone, but

as pigheaded and obstinate as Tutu Lily was when she
was protecting her birds.

She could have told him right off that his experience
on the mainland hadn't prepared him for the Kona
coast—and she would have if he'd asked. But did he?
Of course not. Besides, she had learned a long time ago
that most mainlanders tended to be patronizing—if not
downright disbelieving—when hearing some of the local beliefs. She had been right, of course: he neither
understood *nor* believed. That had been apparent from
the very start.

Of course, she reflected, it wouldn't have made any
difference how he felt about superstitions or myths if he
had been anywhere else. But here on Kona the workers
and almost everyone else *did* believe. And therein lay
the problem.

Liann took another look at the man who, for better
or worse, was her partner for the next few months. Not,
thank God, in a legal, spiritual or marital sense, but in
every other way that counted. No, she realized abruptly,
he wasn't gorgeous. Sexy. She would give him that. Sexy
as all get out. He was also the contractor who had won
the bid to build the large annex to the cultural center on
her home turf, the Big Island of Hawaii.

Eying his substantial frame, which was stiff-backed
with irritation, she allowed herself a quick sigh of self-
pity and muttered, "Why me?" On her next breath, she
answered her own question: because she worked for the
Hawaiian Cultural Institute and she had been assigned
as his interpreter and peacemaker. Furthermore, since
the Center would eventually be her baby, she had decided that whatever it took to make the project run
smoothly she would do. And that, apparently, meant

indoctrinating Cody in the intricacies of "haunted" Hawaii.

And that was taking a lot of work. As she had told the numerous members of her family, it wasn't that he wasn't qualified to build the Center. On the contrary. His company had a well-deserved reputation for building quality hotels. In fact, his recent move from Boston had been made with the intention of adding a few more of them to the already glittering coastline of Waikiki. But first things first. His firm had won the bid for the Center on the Big Island, and three weeks ago, at a meeting of the planning committee, she had met him for the first time.

In a gesture that had already become automatic—as a result of several pointed lectures from Cody—she clapped a hard hat over her long brown hair and stepped out of the office. Approaching him from behind, she stopped several paces away and addressed the back of his head.

"Well, what do you think? Should I call him now?"

"Who?"

"The *kahuna*," she said, gritting her teeth with stoic patience, trying to sound as if she hadn't mentioned the word to him several times a day for the past three weeks. "You know, k-a-h-u—"

Cody turned to face her, his grim gaze moving from the area that, just moments before, had been filled with the deep-throated rumble of machinery. "I know how to spell it," he said, enunciating as clearly as she had. "What I still don't know is why you think we need one of the local priests. I keep reminding you that this is a construction site, not a church."

Liann held up a hand to stop the even flow of words, then changed her mind and swung it in the direction of

his disappearing workers. "It's not going to be anything if you don't get a *kahuna* out here."

"I don't believe this," Cody muttered, staring down
at her. Once again he forcibly reminded himself that size
had nothing to do with anything that mattered. The top
of her head barely came to his chin, but from her shiny
brown hair down to her slim, high-arched feet, she was
one hell of a package. His cupped hand would just fit
over her breast, and the flare of her hips—even in her
modest working shorts—was potent enough to stop a
bulldozer. She shimmered with energy, and her smile
had the voltage of summer lightning. But right now,
those soft pink lips were framing the words he least
wanted to hear.

"Believe it." She reached out with one of her spontaneous gestures and patted his arm with a sympathetic
hand. "Cody, I don't know how to else to say it. It's a
tradition, a formality, to have a *kahuna* bless a new
business or building site." She meticulously avoided
mentioning that to most of the islanders it was a deep-
seated belief, far more than a quaint local custom. He
didn't seem ready for that bit of news.

"And if it isn't blessed?"

Liann watched as Cody ran his hand through his
thick, sun-streaked hair before replacing his hat.

"Well," she said, reluctant to go on, knowing what
his reaction would be. "The workers get uneasy."

"Why?"

"Because some people say that, uh, spirits will,
uh..."

"Will what?"

"Hex the place," she said baldly.

"Oh, for God's sake!"

She tightened her hand on his arm, trying to ignore the play of muscle beneath his warm skin as she slid her thumb over the crisp, burnished hair. When she realized what she was doing, she yanked her hand away and shoved it into the back pocket of her shorts. "Cody, you're not back in Boston, you know. You're in a place where cultures and races have been mixing for generations. A place where everything doesn't come in neatly labeled packages. You have to bend a little."

Cody looked down into the largest, brownest, most extravagantly lashed eyes he'd ever seen. After three weeks they still startled him. "Are you telling me that they believe things like missing equipment and normal mishaps—" his incredulous gesture took in the area so recently vacated by his men, "—are caused by ghosts?"

Liann looked at his exasperated expression. "If you asked them straight out, one-on-one, they'd probably say no." She paused, trying to think like a *haole*, nonnative, someone who hadn't been bred on tales of the supernatural. After a moment she realized it was a lost cause; she could no more get inside of his head than he could hers.

"They'd deny it," she repeated. "But together, as a group, as a *cultural* group," she amended thoughtfully, "yes, they do believe." She saw the protest forming on his face and rushed on before he could interrupt. "Even in this day and age, most of them do. Don't you remember the sign we saw by the river the other day?"

"Which sign?"

"The one that said Cross at Your Own Risk. This Bridge Has Not Been Blessed."

Cody sighed, part of his attention wandering to the hand stuffed in the pocket shaping her rounded bottom, wondering what she would do if he reached out and put it back on his arm. He wanted the touch of her soft fingers again. "I thought it was a joke."

Shaking her head, Liann said simply, "Nobody around here is laughing."

His eyes narrowed as he took in the seriousness of her tone. "I have a feeling I've missed something crucial along the way," he said finally. "This time, I want you to spell it out for me."

It wasn't easy to find the right words, she decided after a moment's thought. She took her time, selecting them with care in her urgency to make him understand.

"Here on the islands, our old people play an important part in our lives. In families where both parents work, the grandparents often step in as a combination of teacher, playmate and adviser. We grow up listening to their stories—the same stories that they heard from their parents and grandparents, who in turn learned the tales from theirs. Stories about the power of nature, of omens and rituals and *kapu*, the forbidden places and things. All this is very real and meaningful to the old people and they've passed their beliefs down to our generation."

"Do *you* believe in them?"

"I could give you a zillion examples of businesses running into trouble when they didn't get the proper blessing," she assured him airily. When he made no sound, encouraging or otherwise, Liann's earnest gaze swung away from him, and she looked out over the piles of fresh earth and abandoned equipment. She really didn't want to watch the speculation in his eyes turn to skepticism. "For instance, hotels have been built and have remained almost empty because tenants complained that they heard people walking through the halls and making noise. But when they checked, no one was there.''

With her expectant gaze on him once more Cody reluctantly said, ''What happened?''

''When the building was properly blessed, all activity stopped. That's just one story. I've got a least a hundred more. Want to hear them?''

Cody shook his head, returning to the subject at hand like a dog worrying a bone. ''I asked if you believe in this stuff.''

''Me?'' she asked with a light laugh, turning away. ''I'm a product of the high-tech generation.''

''That's no answer.''

Liann could feel his eyes all over her, and she took a quick breath as she straightened her spine. How had the early Hawaiians done it? she wondered with heartfelt empathy. They had had the overwhelming task of explaining their various gods to the missionaries, those austere Calvinists who descended on the islands in the early nineteenth century to save the ''heathens.'' Of course, they had had one advantage over her, she consoled herself. The language. The beautiful, musical, deceptively simple Hawaiian language. Deception was an apt description, she decided. Since most of the words had several meanings, it had been duck soup for the courteous islanders to say what the missionaries had wanted to hear and still be true to their own beliefs.

Cody moved a step closer, so near that she felt the heat of his body. ''Well, do you believe or not?''

''There's no quick answer to that. The situation is more complex—''

''Yes or no?''

Liann glared over her shoulder. ''There are a lot of things involved in answering a question like that.''

"Yes or no?" he repeated deliberately, enjoying her look of baffled uncertainty. When all was said and done, he decided, she dithered delightfully.

"Well..."

He waited, a silvery gleam of amusement in his eyes as she drew out the single word.

"Maybe!"

"Maybe? What kind of an answer is that?"

"The only kind you're going to get," she said, beginning to move again.

He reached out, his strong fingers encircling her wrist, bringing her up short. "Wrong, sweetheart. You're going to keep going until I understand what's happening around here." He draped an arm over her shoulders and nudged her toward the shade of a gargantuan tractor.

Liann absently reached up and removed her hat, running her hand through her hair. Cody took the hat from her, replaced it on her head and settled it with a firm tap. He wrapped his fingers around her arm, keeping her next to him.

"Keep that on," he directed, "and quit stalling. I want to hear how today's woman feels about spooks and haunts."

"Well," she said finally, "*this* woman, with her college education and all, tries very hard to be logical and pragmatic. When... disturbances of any kind occur, I *look* for a reasonable answer to the problem."

Her slight hesitation, the careful way she spoke, told Cody far more than she realized. She might hope to, but she didn't always find pat answers, nor did she really expect that she would. His hand tightened fractionally. "What other kind are there?"

Liann shrugged, trying without success to release her arm from his grasp. "Depends on who you talk to. If it happens to be someone like Tutu Lily—"

He interrupted, nodding toward the steep hills behind them. "Our friendly neighborhood bird lady."

Nodding, she continued. "You'd hear another line of reasoning."

"Like what?"

"That perhaps we had offended someone's *aumakua* and this is its way of showing displeasure. That's a personal or family god," she explained when his brows rose in inquiry. "It could be a shark, an owl, almost anything."

"I have a feeling I'm being set up for something, but I'll bite anyway. How do you undo the damage?"

Under the circumstances, her smile was a masterpiece of restraint. "By calling in a *kahuna*."

"Amazing. Why didn't I think of that?" Cody muttered, slumping back against the bright yellow backhoe, taking Liann along with him.

"Don't be sarcastic. You asked, and I'm telling you."

Shelving the subject for the moment, Cody looked around and sighed. "What do you suppose set them off this time?"

Liann shrugged and adjusted her body against the warm metal. For all she knew, it might be as simple as someone whispering that the big eye tuna were running. That was all it would have taken for some of the younger men. "I don't know. You were out here. You tell me."

"One minute they were moving dirt, the next they were gone. JoJo was working the bulldozer—" Cody gestured toward the big yellow tractor "—and he just stopped dead. He jumped down, looked in the hole, called out something and they all took off like skinned cats."

Stepping over to the deep gouge in the red soil, Liann silently looked down. She pointed a slim finger at a smooth ridge that had been made by the slicing metal. "I'll bet that's why."

Cody joined her, his gaze following hers.

"See?" she asked.

He stared down at the newly turned earth. "What?"

Her arm straightened, and she aimed her finger at a small, lumpy object. "That."

He eyed the dirt-encrusted mass. The center of its severed length shone whitely up at him. His skeptical gaze settled on her face, and she nodded.

"You're telling me they left because someone turned up a bone?"

She nodded again, pleased that he had understood. Her smile faltered when his expression grew even grimmer.

"And I suppose you can also tell me why they didn't just come and let me know? They knew I'd check it out, if for no other reason than I'm required to by law."

The soft words were worse than an angry snarl, she decided with a wince. Once again she envied the Old Ones the ability to hide behind a language, to use words that shielded as well as disclosed. However, since she was dealing with a blunt man who laid his cards on the table, and expected others to do the same, she plunged ahead. "Probably they were afraid that this might be an old graveyard. Burial grounds are very sacred to Hawaiians," she explained matter-of-factly. "And frankly, Cody, the men don't have much confidence that you'll respect their ways. So if you *don't*, and that brings trouble, they don't want to be around."

"Why on earth should it bring trouble?"

"To the ancient Hawaiians, bones were sacred. When a man died, his flesh became corrupt, but his immortality lay in his bones." Liann stopped, watching his impassive face. He didn't say a word. She sighed deeply, wondering why she was even trying. "The bones retained the *mana*, the supernatural or divine power of the person. Desecration of the bones means desecration of the spirit. So, even today, no one with any sense messes around with them."

In the silence that followed, Liann wondered what was going on behind Cody's expressionless face. Three weeks wasn't a very long time, especially when it came to understanding such a complex man. He was intelligent; she had known that from the first. He was more thing- than people-oriented. She had learned that the first day they had moved into the field office. While she had been distracted by the comings and goings of the men, he, in the midst of such chaos, had simply withdrawn mentally and pondered the intricacies of his blueprints and schematics.

In the twenty-one days they had worked together, she had decided that he was probably one of the most tenacious men she had ever met. Their current conversation was a prime example. Once his interest was caught, he followed through with the same zeal that a bloodhound displayed while following a scent. Of course, she mused, a man didn't stay at the top of a successful company unless he had a few of the tougher attributes—like self-confidence that bordered on arrogance and a street-smart quality that had nothing at all to do with his upper-crust Boston background.

But how were his instincts? she wondered. Would he be able to set aside all of his know-how, turn his back on the rational and be a part of a ceremony that was completely alien to him? Because more than permission for the ritual would be demanded of him; nothing less than wholehearted approval would be required to satisfy the doubts of his crew.

So absorbed was she in her evaluation, she almost missed the answer to her questions.

"Oh, hell," Cody sighed, "go call him."

"Who?" she asked with a startled blink.

"The *kahuna*."

The next afternoon, Cody sat behind his desk mentally listing the symptoms of advanced island fever. Obviously that's what he had. It was the only way he could account for the unusual activity outside. Or the only explanation he was willing to accept. He was so accustomed to the noise, he barely heard the straining machines scooping and depositing large amounts of dirt as they leveled the uneven ground. The men were back, every last one of them, their smiles open and amiable. He shifted impatiently, knowing that they felt as if they had won both the battle *and* the war.

As far as he knew, no one had informed them that the blessing would take place first thing that morning. Regardless, they had all been there. Probably notified by jungle drums, he decided wryly. Or conch shells. Whatever. Considering the logistics of reaching them by other means, it was as good an explanation as any.

The *kahuna* had surprised him. He had expected a hollow-eyed mystic; what he got was a congenial minister with a thatch of steel-gray hair who had blended old and new traditions into a surprisingly palatable ceremony. Liann had called him uncle. Uncle Loe. Cody didn't know why he was surprised. Apparently she was related to half the people on the island—and on very good terms with the other half.

Deliberately shifting his thoughts away from her, he considered the ceremony that had taken place earlier that day. It had been conducted almost entirely in Hawaiian, and had included a lot of chanting. He hadn't understood one word in ten. Not that it made a lot of difference—he apparently hadn't been expected to contribute to the event. His job, as he understood it, was to be receptive and approving, and to look as if the whole thing was his idea. It hadn't been difficult. In fact, the entire procedure had been unexpectedly painless. But what had impressed him most was the effect it had on the crew. Construction workers in general, and this group in particular, had a reputation as hell-raisers. As far as his workers went, it was well deserved. But this morning the men had been solemn and, yes, reverent. Afterward, their main emotion had been unadulterated relief. It had been apparent in their grins and buoyant comments as they had returned to work.

He frowned as he thought of one additional result: their interest in Liann had resurfaced—in spades. Right from the start, she hadn't been able to walk across the yard without several of them trying to move in on her. Even with his back turned, the whistles and frank comments had told him exactly where she was. As if he'd needed them, he thought in disgust. His antenna worked overtime where she was concerned. He always knew when she was within fifty feet of him.

His scowl darkened when he picked up a pencil to initial the paper on his desk and bore down so hard that the lead broke. It wasn't as if she encouraged the men. She simply drew them, like bees to honey. Their attentions had tapered off noticeably while the men were occupied with troublesome spirits, but now everything was back to normal. After the blessing, a cluster of them went out of their way to talk to her before returning to work. Talk, hell! They swarmed all over her, teasing, touching. And Kai, the brawny foreman, had bent his head and kissed her. Cody's eyes narrowed at the memory. The only reason he hadn't interfered was because of Liann's reaction to the caress. Or, rather, the lack of it. She had merely laughed up at the tall man and informed him that it was time to get to work.

He was spending an inordinate amount of time thinking about Liann, Cody reflected, settling back in his chair, a grim set to his mouth. Especially for a man whose personal blueprint didn't call for serious involvement with a woman, any woman, during the next two years. At least that had been the plan. And his life, for more years than he cared to count, had been successfully centered around such plans. He had achieved most of what he'd set out to accomplish. The things he hadn't, he'd decided somewhere along the way, weren't really important. Having learned the value of goals and timelines, he now did very little on impulse.

When Terry Tanaka, his former college roommate, asked him to consider working in the islands, he had evaluated the offer in his usual manner: methodically and with meticulous attention to details. When it came right down to it, though, there hadn't been that much to consider. They were both successful contractors, so a partnership, even if it was only temporary, would be mutually advantageous, allowing them to be more aggressive in seeking new business. There were no personal reasons why he should stay based in the east; he could always fly back to Boston to visit his family. As he saw it, in a couple of years they'd pretty much be home free. Two years of dedicating all their time and energy to work and they could write their own tickets.

That was the plan, and it seemed simple enough. Until the day of the planning committee meeting when he'd looked down into the most candid brown eyes he'd ever seen. Just a few inches below those eyes were lips that curved in a smile that rocked him back on his heels. And the rest of Liann Murphy? That was simple enough. Every time he was around her, he had to fight to keep his hands to himself. And as each day passed, he came closer to losing the battle.

She would never make a living as a model. She wasn't actually beautiful, he told himself thoughtfully, trying to inject a note of objectivity into his self-indulgent fantasies. Nor was she tall and willowy with dramatic cheekbones. However, if an agent were looking for someone cuddly and feminine, with eyes like a fawn, to sell, say, milk or baby shampoo, she'd be a gold mine. She had a wholesome allure that incited men to dream of home and hearth and a clutch of kids. And the amazing thing about it was that she didn't have the slightest inkling that she left every male within a radius of twenty feet stumbling over their own feet and bumping into things.

Not to say that she was dim. Quite the opposite, as a matter of fact. Cody got up and stepped over to the window, his gaze quite naturally settling on Liann, who waved and smiled at a cluster of men as she headed toward the office. A sudden frown carved deep lines around his eyes as he considered her animated expression. No, if he had to make a guess at what made Liann Murphy tick, he'd say that she'd had a bad experience with a man somewhere along the way that had left her very, very cautious. No attractive woman of twenty-five could be that unaware of her impact on men. Especially not if she was surrounded by them ten hours a day. Something—and he'd give a lot to know what it was—had made her opt for the role of friendly confidante, deliberately smothering her normal sexual instincts.

He was still brooding about that when she threw open the door and stepped up into the trailer, bringing sunlight and the fragrance of flowers with her.

"What do you think?"

His gaze took in her hair, which was pulled up off her neck with a curved turquoise clip, and then moved to the matching cotton jumpsuit that faithfully followed the tantalizing curves of her body. "About what?" he asked absently.

"The blessing, of course." What else? she wondered, her eyes widening in faint alarm. The way he was examining her, you might think she'd asked for an opinion on her bikini panties and bra.

"It was okay."

"Okay? That's it? *Okay?* It was the best one I've ever been to."

"Since I understood very little, I'm obviously not much of a judge," he said laconically. "I'll take your word for it."

"Do that. All our troubles are over," she blithely assured him. "Uncle Loe didn't miss a trick. There isn't a ghost or spirit around that would dare kick up a fuss now."

Before Liann's lips closed over the last word, someone pounded an imperious tattoo on the door.

Cody's fingers threaded through his thick hair in exasperation. "Too bad your uncle didn't include something to counteract the substantial lady on the hill. I'd recognize that thump anywhere. Better open the door before she breaks it down."

Liann grimaced. "She's only trying to protect her birds."

He nodded grimly. "Sure, at the cost of this entire project. Let her in."

"Remember," Liann whispered, "she's just an old lady."

"She's a pain in the— Never mind. Let her in and we'll listen to her latest complaint."

Chapter Two

Tutu Lily, who was swathed in a bright floral muu-muu, entered, and nodded serenely at Cody before accepting his invitation to be seated.

Even though he knew the next few minutes were going to be a hard lesson in exasperation, Cody forced himself to relax and let the two women handle the preliminary amenities. This was the old woman's third visit—she turned up on a weekly basis.

She didn't like anything about the building under construction—whether it was the site, the height, or the size of it—and she came on a regular basis to register her complaints. She had no argument with the purpose of the Center; she simply didn't want it in her front yard. He had finally pried out of her the fact that she lived more than a mile away, but in her estimation it wasn't far enough. During the first visit, Cody had patiently explained that the site was nowhere near her property line. It was at that point that he had learned she had a rather skewed, if generous, mind-set when it came to interpreting where her boundaries ended and the Institute's began.

Her voice had been rich and unhurried, and she had kept her words deliberately simple, just in case the round-eyed white man had difficulty understanding the way things were on the islands. Although she was polite, her underlying belief had come across loud and clear: more often than not, *haoles* were a bit thick.

Now, while the two women discussed the weather as a prelude to the main event, Cody winced as he recalled the first interrogation Lily had conducted. It had, he'd decided later, been her version of an ordinary conversation. Her part had been to ask questions, his to nod in agreement.

He knew that she lived at the top of the hill, yeh?

Nod.

She waved a hand approximately the size of a ham hock and made a circle above her head as she voiced the next question. There was air all around her house, yeh?

Nod.

Air between her and the ocean, yeh?

Nod.

Everybody has their own air, yeh?

Nod.

Her air was around her place, his air was around his, yeh?

Nod.

If that was so, and he even *agreed* it was so, then why did the Institute plan a building that had parts of it sticking up in *her* air, between her house and the ocean?

That was when he tried to explain the concept that construction was tied primarily to land, not the air. Besides, he wondered aloud, what about the Institute's space? She looked at him in pity, pointedly ignoring his question. Everyone, she stated, knew that you didn't put things up in someone else's air, or block that person's view. It wasn't polite. Besides, in this case, it bothered her birds. She wanted the Institute to change their plans. Move. Go somewhere else. Right away. And with that, she had risen majestically, moving smoothly despite her ample proportions.

Yes, ample was an apt word, he decided, putting aside the memories of that first visit and allowing his gaze to drift over the imposing woman. Everything about her was generous. A thick braid of white hair, which was usually secured atop her head with what looked like a lethal chopstick, fell almost to her hips. When she stood, her brown eyes looked straight into his, which put her at a couple of inches over six feet, and she outweighed him by more than a hundred pounds. Yet, when she wasn't battering at his door with the side of her large fist, she moved with stately grace.

"Tutu Lily wants to know if anything's being done about the complaints she made last week," Liann said, interrupting his reflections. Her polite, businesslike tone belied the glimmer of humor in her eyes.

Cody's gaze met hers for an instant, and he savored the amused "here we go again" message that flowed between them. Moments of intimate communion with a woman whose eyes gleamed with feminine mischief were rare in his life. He could, he decided, become easily addicted to them—and to her.

Turning to the older woman, he decided to use her own tactics and resort to short, blunt words. Any other method was just inviting complications; she had a way of taking a normal conversation and twisting things to her advantage within thirty seconds. At any given time her verbal style was a bewildering combination of the enigmatic, poetic and, when it suited her, abrupt.

"I've checked the changes you proposed with the planning committee, but I can't offer you any encouragement," he told her, then waited for some response. When she remained silent, watching him expectantly, he closed his eyes for an instant, realizing that this visit wasn't going to run any smoother than the first two.

"First of all, I met with the committee and, just as I expected, I was told that the Center can't be moved to another location. The Institute owns the property and none of it intrudes onto your boundary lines. As a matter of fact, it doesn't even come close. Next, the plans of the structure have been sanctioned, so they can't be changed. What that means is that your request to have the roof lowered has been denied. I *have* talked to the men about being more quiet. Since they know how concerned you are about your birds, they've tried, but bulldozers and backhoes are noisy machines, and there's not much we can do about them." He leaned back and waited again. No change of expression crossed the old woman's face. "Have I forgotten anything?" he finished politely.

Liann settled back in her chair. This could be the battle of the century, she told herself, biting back a smile at the sight of the stubborn man and woman each trying to outstare the other. Cody was going to be civil if it killed him. And Auntie Lily? She would grab a shield and spear and tear through the place like one of King Kamehameha's warriors if she thought it would help.

Of course, the old woman had a lot at stake, Liann reflected. In an effort to attract birds and offer them a place of safety, she had followed the precedent set by her ancestors and had left the acreage around the family home lush and untouched. Amazingly enough, the birds seemed to realize that the area was a sanctuary and settled there in droves. Auntie talked to them as if they were children, greeted new flocks with welcoming chants and sped migrating birds on their way with loud and protracted blessings. She fed them, pampering the weak and injured, and her wrath was impressive if anyone pestered them. She was not taking kindly to a construction crew, complete with snorting and clanking machinery, coming anywhere near her babies!

"No, Cody Hunter, your memory is excellent," Lily told him after a pause, tilting her head in a regal nod after perceptibly ticking off on her fingers each item of complaint as Cody spoke. She waited until his broad shoulders relaxed against the back of his chair before commenting. "But you bring back the wrong answer."

Cody's fingers tugged at his thick hair in an absent gesture of frustration. Stopping at his nape, he massaged the knots of tension as he examined the woman's bland expression. Did she really have royal blood? he wondered. Rumor had it, or so Liann said, that Lily was of the *alii*, the nobility. He sighed wearily, wondering what the penalty would be for getting rid of a queen-size pest—especially if it was one whose lineage might just match her proportions.

"I was responsible for the questions, not the answers," he reminded her. "I had nothing to do with the committee's decision."

Lily shook her head, disagreeing. "Not so," she told him. "You had more to do with it than you know."

"How?"

"Bad thoughts," she said, dragging out the first word to emphasize the iniquity of it all.

Cody's gaze slid to Liann's face, mutely asking if he had heard what he *thought* he'd heard. She raised her brows before looking away from him, obviously knowing what Lily had in mind and not wanting to be part of it.

"Are you saying," he challenged the older woman, "that it's my fault they said no?"

Lily nodded. Liann cleared her throat.

"What did you think inside your head when you told the men about the changes I want?" Lily demanded.

Disbelief darkened Cody's gray gaze as he absorbed the staccato words. "Think? I don't know. I suppose I figured that they'd say no. That I'd be lucky if they didn't laugh me out of the room." Besides, he hadn't *wanted* them to change their minds. He intended to put the building up according to the original plans.

Lily's shrug clearly said, *What did I tell you?* "See," she told the room at large. "All wrong. Very bad thoughts."

"What was I supposed to be thinking about?" Cody asked curiously, forgetting that he had planned to say his piece and hustle her out of the room.

"My birds," Lily said, taking him literally.

"How would that help?"

Liann shifted restlessly, drawing Cody's attention to her carefully blank face. When she obstinately refused to look at him, his gaze returned to the other woman.

"You need more than words," Lily told him. "You need pictures—lotsa good pictures—in your head. You think and think and think them."

"Pictures," he repeated, not even making it a question. She was going to do it now, he thought grimly, rubbing the back of his neck again to stop the creeping tension before it settled in for good. He could feel it in

his bones. Any second now she would close her eyes and
start that infernal chanting. Right before his eyes, she
would...what? He didn't know if it was a rare bit of
showmanship, or if she actually called on some mysterious power; whatever she did, he didn't like it. It wasn't
cut-and-dried the way he preferred things. When he
encountered Lily, he always had the feeling that he was
dealing with more than one woman, and that was pro-
foundly disturbing. "Pictures," he muttered again.

She nodded, her heavily lashed eyes closing and her
voice falling into a gently singsong rhythm. "You must
form a clear picture in your mind, Cody Hunter, of my
house. My *lanai*. Make the image clear, in great detail,
all during the day. From the early light when the birds
have not yet called to each other until darkness stills
their cries. Watch, as in the light of the falling gold, I
follow the yellow bird. I watch its flight until at last it
sleeps." She stopped, opened her eyes and waited, just
looking at him.

Cody didn't nod or give any other indication that he
understood. If she was going to be cryptic, he could be
stubborn. Fair was fair. "That's it? I picture you on
your porch—your *lanai*?"

Tutu Lily nodded again, and her voice grew softer
still. "Until the flight of the bird is done. So long as the
golden light gleams, I watch it. So long as the golden
light gleams, I bless it." There was silence in the room
until, finally, Lily heaved herself to her feet. "That's
what you tell the men when you see them next time,"
she directed in her normal voice. "I be back next week,
Cody Hunter."

Before she had taken more than a couple of steps,
Cody said, "It's a little hard to picture a house and a
porch that I've never seen." Lily's sudden smile re-

minded him of his fifth grade teacher, a woman whose expression thawed only when one of her students displayed exceptional brilliance.

"Auwe!" she said in a forgiving tone, apparently struck by his logic. "That was why. Bad wisdom, not bad thoughts!" Pointing a beefy finger at Liann, she ordered, "In three days you bring him to my place. Should be sooner so he can make the pictures, but I am very, very busy. A buncha new birds coming in. After lunch in three days. Remember!"

At the soft sound of the closing door, Cody blinked and turned to Liann. "Is that good or bad?"

"Did you have to get her started?" she demanded in exasperation, leaving her chair and moving over to the window. She stood moodily staring until Lily was out of sight.

Cody stepped behind her, his large hands dropping to her shoulders. "Get her started on what?" He watched as the afternoon sun brought out red highlights in her shining fall of hair, ignoring the implied accusation.

At the feel of his fingers flexing through the light material of her knit shirt, Liann drew a shaky breath. She wanted nothing to do with a man like Cody—a man who knew so little about her way of life and understood even less. So far, her track record wasn't all that hot, she reminded herself: one mercifully short marriage to a man who was as charming as he was deluded. He'd actually expected to separate her from the very elements of life that made her exactly what she was.

Involuntarily she shifted, and Cody tightened his grip fractionally. His hands were large and warm, and his thumbs kneaded small circles between her shoulders, touching the spots that coiled with tension. Realizing, belatedly, that both the man and his strong, competent touch could become habit-forming, she shrugged and started to move away. In less time than it took to think about it, she was hemmed in between the window and his hard body. Barely moving, he shifted his weight and gently tightened his fingers. The result was the same as if he had chained her to the spot: she couldn't move an inch.

"Uh, Cody..."

"Started what, Liann?" His voice was gentle, but his taut body told her he wasn't about to let her go. "Tell me about it."

A tremor ran through her, and she knew he felt it. She *felt* him feel it, was aware of the blanket of male satisfaction settling around her. Rattled by his closeness and her own reactions, she took a deep breath and concentrated. He wanted to know what Lily was up to, she reminded herself. Wanted to know about the pictures. Right. "I suppose anything you'd find on the self-help shelves in a bookstore would call it visualizations," she told him.

"Sounds safe enough," he commented, drawing her closer and easing her back against his chest. "I haven't read about the process, but I know that there have been books out about it for some time. I've seen them. Seems harmless enough to me."

"Creative visualization," she said briskly, "is using your imagination to create what you want in life. It's harnessing your natural power of imagination to the basic energy of the universe. It's the latest thing in motivational and self-help techniques. It's also potent and, if done correctly, enormously effective."

"So?"

"The *kahunas* have used it since the beginning of time," she said gently.

Cody turned her around to face him. "Are you trying to tell me that the bird lady is a—"

"I'm just saying it's a possibility."

"I doubt it."

She slanted a glance up at him, intrigued by his assured tone. "Why?"

"Well, for one thing she doesn't look like one."

"Ah. Exactly what does one look like?"

"For starters," he said warily, blinking at her brilliant smile, "not like my Aunt Hattie dressed in a muumuu and thonged sandals."

"Aunt Hattie?"

"The skeleton in the Hunter closet who holds conversations with flowers and butterflies."

Liann smiled and tried to step away, only to be gently brought back into the fold of his arms. "Interesting," she said, arching her back to keep her lips from touching the warm skin at the open neck of his khaki shirt. "But if she lived over here, she probably *would* be one."

"What difference does it make?"

"Maybe a lot," she said thoughtfully.

And that, he gathered from her abstracted tone, was all he was going to get out of her. He reluctantly released her and spent the rest of the afternoon watching as she moved restlessly from one window to another or sat at her desk, tracing doodles on a pad of paper.

Liann's fidgeting was contagious. He couldn't concentrate on the blueprints before him, so he pulled out some paper and scrawled a note to Sammy, their phlegmatic night watchman. Liann had said to be sure to tell him about the blessing and that the bone found earlier was from a dog, not a human. After slipping it into an envelope, he looked up and said, "What's the matter?"

"Nothing," she mumbled, frowning at a stack of reference books piled on a corner of her desk. When she finally reached for one, he noted that it was a thick tome on Hawaiian folklore. That in itself wasn't unusual, he reflected, especially since one aspect of her job at the Institute was to research and document old myths and legends. He just didn't like the way she pored over it after each one of Lily's visits.

She opened the book, ran a finger down the table of contents, flipped to a page and was immediately absorbed. So absorbed that she didn't notice that he had given up all pretense of being busy and was watching her. She had far more than just an academic interest in the book, he noted grimly. Something was bothering her—something about Lily and the birds—and she was definitely not planning to share her concern with him.

Of course, he couldn't blame her. Ever since he'd begun the job he'd been floundering around like the proverbial fish out of water. For a man who had no trouble dealing with the usual crises that came with the building trade, he was out of his element in an atmosphere of ghostly tales and traditions.

"Liann."

"Ummm?"

"What are you doing?"

Without looking in his direction, she checked the front of the book and jotted down some page numbers. "Nothing," she mumbled.

He waited with mounting impatience as she fanned some pages and stopped, reading the chapter heading. Muttering beneath her breath, she skipped to another section and scanned several pages. She flipped through some more, stopping several times. Finally she slammed down the heavy cover of the book and stared straight ahead.

"It's not here," she said to the wall. Her tone held no surprise.

"What isn't?"

With a start, she turned her gaze toward Cody. "Nothing important," she said vaguely, lifting the heavy book and placing it back on the stack. "Just checking an idea I had, but I must have been wrong." Before he could interrupt, she changed the subject abruptly. "Are you still coming to the house tonight?" The idea wasn't hers; she'd done her best to keep him out of her personal life. The invitation had come from her parents.

He leaned back in his chair and laced his fingers behind his head, studying the look of uneasy guilt on her face. "If you don't want to tell me something," he advised evenly, "just tell me to butt out. You can't lie worth a damn. Are you sure your folks won't mind?" he continued without a break.

"You've been invited," she reminded him, deciding not to argue about her evasive answer. She had known for years that if she wanted to conceal something, she should wear a paper bag over her head. "That's more than most people get. Things are pretty loose at our place, and tonight there's going to quite a crowd. We have a large family and most of them will probably be drifting in and out," she explained when his heavy brows rose questioningly.

"What's the occasion?"

Liann shook her head. "There is none. That's just the way things are at our house."

"Okay," he said with a slow nod, "thanks, I'll be there. I'll bring some wine. What time?"

"Six-thirty or seven. It doesn't really matter. We operate on Hawaiian time."

"Which means?" Cody asked, an expectant gleam in his smoky eyes.

"That when an event is ready, it happens."

She had been right on all counts, Cody decided at about nine-thirty that evening. Dinner was an event and had happened at a little after eight. More than half of his crew was there—cousins, Liann had explained succinctly. Even Kai, the foreman, which explained her attitude about the kiss.

Her immediate family was large; she was one of seven children. Her father, Sean, was a redheaded giant who had emigrated from Ireland with two carbon-copy brothers. The three of them had gladly traded an island torn by strife and icy winter storms for one that was warmed by the trade winds and an occasional volcanic eruption. Each had married an island woman and sired a large and colorful brood of children.

Mei, Liann's mother, had the serene beauty and strength needed to tame a turbulent Celt. Liann's brothers and sisters were a mixed batch, ranging from the older ones with deep brown skin, hair and eyes to the two youngest, Megan and Devin, who had flaming red hair and bright blue eyes. Liann, he noted with possessive satisfaction, had skin like warm honey, and fell just about in the middle. She was also raising his blood pressure with that off-the-shoulder, blue-flowered thing she was wearing.

The house was as unexpected and intriguing as the family. It had been remodeled in stages until it was more

a Polynesian fantasy compound than a single structure. An open-air patio extended from the house and led
out to the swimming pool. Cody followed a walk that
wound past gardens of tropical plants to one of the
guest cottages. The thatched roof of fire-treated cane,
Sean had told him, was widely used in Fiji because of its
wearability. Much of the complex had been built on the
island plan, using screens instead of walls so that they
could take advantage of the trade winds and sunlight.
Back beyond the pool was a large combination office
and master bedroom retreat Sean had built so that he
and Mei could have some privacy. A twisting pathway
led visitors past miniature waterfalls, cascading foun-
tains, ponds and lacy ferns. Cane and white rattan furniture with colorful cushions provided bright conversational areas, both inside and out.

"Found you! How come you're wandering around
out here all by yourself?"

Cody turned, an indulgent smile curving his lips as a
red-haired sprite linked her arm through his. "It's a bit
of a busman's holiday," he confessed. "I couldn't resist looking at the design. Your dad did a wonderful job
with this, Megan."

"Are you taking notes? Going to expand on the idea
and create some hot hotel complex?" Megan tilted her
head and shot a teasing glance up at him. "Good. That
might keep you around for a while."

Her smile had the same voltage as Liann's, he noted
with one part of his mind. And as soon as she discovered that her feminine magic didn't depend upon tor-
menting looks and tantalizing comments, she'd have the
same understated sensuality. And God help the man
who decided to claim her.

"How old are you?" he asked, smoothly changing direction and leading her back to the patio.

"Old enough?" she said hopefully.

Cody's laugh was a rumbling chuckle of pure amusement. Her wide-eyed, outrageously expectant look told him all he needed to know. The little torch top thought she was safe and was playing for all she was worth. Hell, she'd probably taken one look at his response to Liann and *known* she was safe. The kid was trying her wings, but she'd run so fast her pretty little sarong would unwind if he so much as made a move in her direction.

"Not for me," he assured her, reaching out and tugging gently on a lock of her hair that was resting on one slim shoulder. "But if I'm still hanging around in five years..."

"You won't be," she said with sudden seriousness as they neared the others.

"You sound awfully sure of yourself." He raised his voice to be heard over the sound of the various conversations.

Her smile was back. "I am. Didn't you know? Devin and I see all, hear all, know all. My twin and I are the family prophets." She looked around until she spotted her sister. "Hey, Liann! Look who I found wandering around in the dark. You have to take better care of him than that."

Cody grasped at her slim wrist as she slipped away into the crowd and found his hand claimed by Liann. She looked up at him, studying his expression.

"All right," she sighed, "what did she say to put that look on your face?"

"Prophets? What else do you have besides hexes and rituals, nightly séances?"

"Drat the girl," she said in resignation. "She's in one of her fey moods tonight. Don't pay any attention. Really. We're a nice, normal family, and we do nice, normal things."

Cody's skepticism was obvious. "What did she mean?" he asked, watching over the heads of others until the flaming hair disappeared.

Liann tucked her arm into his and steered him in the direction of the pool. She was aware that she couldn't have budged him if he hadn't chosen to go. There was something about his deliberate strength that told her when Cody elected to remain in one place, he would be as immovable as a boulder. "Okay," she said finally, "just what did she say?"

"Nothing much. Only that she and Devin were the family prophets."

Groaning, Liann said, "By the time the twins came along, the Murphy men decided that the Hawaiian influence on the family was a bit top-heavy. The kids didn't have a chance."

Cody broke her thoughtful silence. Enjoying the touch of her body brushing against his, he folded his hand over hers to keep her close and asked, "How so?"

"Well, besides the traditional stuff my mother's family passed on, the twins got a triple dose of Irish folklore. The usual elves and leprechauns were thrown in with smatterings of banshees and people with the 'sight.'"

"Good lord! It's a wonder those kids ever survived."

"They've had a wonderful life. The best of both worlds, you might say." She nudged him slightly to the left, toward the edge of the wandering, free-form pool.

"*You* might. I wouldn't," he pointed out. He looked around, selected a wicker love seat and sat down, bringing her down beside him. "I'm much more conventional."

"I've noticed," she said dryly. Then, in a tone meant to offer comfort, she added, "But you're amazingly flexible. Just look at what you've done since you've been here."

He tucked a wandering strand of hair behind her ear so that he could have an unobstructed view of her profile. "Like what?"

Liann tilted her head consideringly. "Well, you've endured the planning committee meetings without exploding, you've learned a lot about the men working for you, you haven't been intimidated by Auntie Lily and you've met a *kahuna* and experienced a blessing!"

"That's it?" His brows rose in inquiry.

"Isn't it enough?"

"You've forgotten one thing."

"What?"

His hand cupped her bare shoulder and he looked down at her uplifted face. "Not forgotten, actually, you never knew."

"What?"

"Of course, you didn't know because I didn't tell you."

"*What*, for heaven's sake?"

"About a decision I made."

"About what?" she said through gritted teeth.

"That I want you."

Chapter Three

Want? Liann thought, dazed. *Want?* How? And Where? In his office? No, he already had her there. In his rented condo? In his arms? In his bed? One thing was sure, she thought wryly, if she didn't put a stop to the kind of visualizations in which *she* had been indulging lately, any of those options were possible! They may have been involuntary, and quite against her better judgment, but they definitely were erotic.

"Want?" she finally croaked. Clearing her throat, she said, "You shouldn't go around saying things like that."

Cody shifted, drawing her closer. "Why not? It's the truth."

They were sitting so close together that she couldn't put a hand between them to brace herself, so she used his thigh. Pressing down on it, she eased out from under his arm and edged away until she could lean against the back of the love seat. "At the very least, it lacks a certain finesse,'' she complained mildly, glancing up at him, determined to handle the situation with a light touch.

She was simply not going to allow smoky, seductive eyes to rush her into something she would regret for the rest of her life. Nor would she allow the rest of his potent packaging to persuade her. She had based one such decision on a charming facade and had learned a painful lesson: she needed much more than a superficial relationship; she needed depth and commitment, something she had never found with Del. She wouldn't make the same mistake twice.

Of course, she thought with a wry smile, no one with an ounce of sense would call Cody charming. Everything about him was blunt, aggressive and a bit hard-edged. Even the clothes he wore reflected his no-nonsense approach to life. His solid blue shirt, several shades lighter than his slacks, and his gleaming cordovan loafers, were a distinct contrast to the wild floral shirts, shorts and sneakers that most of the other men wore. His only concession to the occasion was to roll up his shirt cuffs several times.

In the beginning, he had, reluctantly, deferred to her judgment at times, but that was because he was in unfamiliar territory. With each passing day, she could see the changes in him; he was settling in, slowly but surely taking control. And that was fine on the job, she allowed. He was expected to exert his authority there. But if anything ever developed between them, that would be a different story. She was not handing the running of her life over to anyone, ever again.

With a deliberation that was vaguely threatening, Cody reached over and softly snared her earlobe between his thumb and forefinger. Stroking her gently, he murmured, "You surprise me. I didn't think finesse was high on anyone's list around here. No one on the crew bothers with it, Lily's method is more of the iron fist in an armored glove, and you shoot pretty straight from the shoulder."

With a breathless laugh, Liann tried to edge farther away before she melted all over him. Did he know what he was doing to her with that feathery touch? she wondered. When his hand lightly brushed against her cheek, she shivered and involuntarily glanced up. Sucking in a breath at the look of his gleaming gray eyes, she knew she had never seen determination like that before. He wasn't joking, she realized. The man was deadly serious! Aside from that, he knew *exactly* what he was doing to her. "I thought that's how you preferred to deal with people," she finally said, once she was sure that her voice wouldn't shake. "No pussyfooting around."

"Exactly." His smile reeked of male satisfaction. "So I wonder why you expect subtlety about something so important."

Startled, she looked up, meeting his gaze. "Is it? Important, I mean."

"Very."

"We've only known each other a few weeks," she protested, wondering when he had moved closer. It wasn't her imagination; he was definitely hemming her in.

"I know exactly how long it's been. I also know that you have fifty or sixty well-meaning relatives who are eventually going to start bringing home men for you to meet."

Liann stiffened. "So?"

"I want my claim to be established before that happens," he told her calmly.

"*Claim?* I'm not some land parcel in a gold rush, for heaven's sake! I'm a woman."

"I know."

His quiet voice stilled the rest of her complaint. And if that hadn't done it, the expression on his face would have, she decided after a second glance. She had the disoriented feeling of one who had reached down to pet a kitten and had been met by the gaze of a fully aroused lion. The look on his face almost took her breath away. She had become accustomed to his more controlled glances, she realized in dismay. Even though she had suspected that he had umplumbed depths, she wasn't prepared to cope with them. She didn't even *want* to. Her plans did not include tangling with a man who went all out to get what he wanted—especially if what he wanted was her!

"No," she stated firmly, shaking her head to emphasize the point. "Absolutely not. It won't work."

"What won't?"

Liann glared at him, her frustration evident even in the flickering light of the torches that surrounded the pool. "Whatever you're trying to cook up between us. There must be several hundred women on this side of the island who would die for your attention, but I..." She paused, thinking frantically, then settled gratefully for the first thought that popped into her head. "I never mix business and pleasure," she finished on a triumphant note.

"I told you before," he said dryly, "that you're a rotten liar. There's no problem with that, and you know it. I'm going to do my job, and I know you'll do yours. But," he added equably, "it *is* encouraging when you admit that whatever happens between us will be a pleasure. I'm glad you understand that much."

"Cody? Liann?" At the soft call, first from one of her parents, then from the other, the two of them got up and turned.

"Over here." Cody's deep voice overrode hers. "By the pool." Liann took a step back, grateful for the interruption even as part of her mind wondered what outrageous thing he would have come up with next.

Sean and Mei stepped out of the shadows. "You have a telephone call," Sean said, narrowing his eyes as he absorbed his daughter's tense figure and the casual assurance of the man standing at her side.

"Which one of us is it for?" Liann asked, moving toward the older couple and coming to an abrupt halt when Cody's fingers closed around her wrist. His loose grasp wasn't painful. Just confining, she discovered when she tugged and found that instead of releasing her he closed the distance between them and slid his hand down, calmly threading his fingers through hers.

"Either one, or both," Mei said serenely, one eyebrow raised slightly at her daughter's poorly concealed agitation. "It's Sammy."

"Sammy?" Liann's gaze swung to Cody, their minor skirmish forgotten. Sammy Lin, the night watchman, was a small, wiry, fearless man skilled in various forms of the martial arts—and a person who preferred to handle his own problems. Knowing that he wouldn't call under ordinary circumstances, she frowned. Turning back to her mother, she asked, "Does he sound all right?"

Mei tilted her head and considered the question. "Flustered," she said finally. She looked up at her husband, waiting for his nod of agreement. "Flustered," she repeated.

"Where's the closest phone?" Cody asked Sean after a quick glance at Liann's face.

"Use our office."

Cody nodded, took a firmer grasp on the small hand in his and said, "Let's go." They rushed through the office door and Cody lifted the receiver, motioning for Liann to move closer so she could hear. When their heads were nearly touching he said, "Sammy? What's up?"

"Your note said you had the place blessed this morning!"

The curious statement was not just a casual pleasantry, Cody decided, staring down at the phone. He had heard a number of pointed accusations in his lifetime, and this definitely fell in that category.

"Sammy," Liann interrupted, "what's the matter?"

"Did you or didn't you?"

"Of course we did. Uncle Loe did it."

"Then you'd better give him a call, because he left out a chunk."

Liann looked at Cody in bewilderment. He didn't know Sammy all that well, so he didn't realize how atypical the conversation was. The unflappable old man was practically incoherent. "What are you talking about, Sammy. What's *wrong*?"

"What's wrong is that I'm locked up in your trailer with two desks in front of the door and I'm not coming out until daylight!"

Wrapping her hand around Cody's to get the receiver closer to her ear, Liann practically shrieked, "Why? What's happening? Have you called the police?"

"Won't do any good," Sammy said fatalistically. "This place is crawling with night marchers."

Liann sat looking out the window as Cody's BMW tore down the darkened road, its lights leaping ahead to stab at the darkness. She had watched his hands on the steering wheel until his ominous silence had stretched her nerves to the breaking point. So she waited, wishing he would say something, *anything*, and then winced when he finally did. The restrained violence in his voice told her that he wanted an answer, a reasonable one, and he wanted it right now. The problem was, she thought, that she didn't have one that fit in that category. In fact, she didn't have one that he would even come close to buying.

"So, give. Who exactly are—what did you call them—the marchers of the night?"

"Uh, maybe *what* they are is a better question," she said in a small voice.

Cody's oath was stark, sibilant and succinct.

"Some people say," she began cautiously, "that they're *alii* ghosts—you know, the royal families—who march at night."

Cody's language didn't improve.

"There are several ways they can be identified," she persevered, wondering if she was doomed to a future of explaining extraordinary things to a man who clearly thought she had slipped a cog or two.

"What or who can be identified?" Cody demanded.

"The spirits," she said patiently.

The car veered sharply to the right, then straightened. "Do I really want to know this?" he asked in sudden resignation.

"I think so." He'd better hear it from her now, she decided, because heaven only knew what Sammy would have to say. And she'd bet her latest edition of *Folk Tales: Fact or Fantasy?* that it was going to be pretty spectacular. Sammy Lin was one tough old bird, and it took a lot to rattle him.

"The usual warnings go something like this," she instructed evenly, staring straight ahead. "If you're out on a moonless night—and you'll notice, by the way, that there is no moon tonight—and see flickering lights coming your way...run!"

"You really believe this, don't you?"

"You asked and I'm telling you. Now, let me finish. It's even worse if you hear voices and soft laughter. And most dangerous of all is if the voices and lights are accompanied by the distant throb of drums."

"Oh, my God. What if people are out walking with flashlights?"

"You've missed the point," she said patiently. "You see lights and hear voices, but there are no people. Anyway," she ended abruptly as he swung into the dirt parking lot, "it's the worst kind of bad luck to cross their path. Nothing but death and disaster will follow."

"So what do you do if you just innocently get in their way?" he asked with morbid fascination.

"Exactly what Sammy did. You skedaddle and hide."

"Come on," Cody said, killing the motor and pocketing the key. "Let's go get him. I want to show him that there's nothing out here."

Liann opened her door and slipped out before he could get around to her side. "I'm right behind you, but I warn you, if I see or hear anything suspicious, I'm jumping right in there with Sammy!"

"What happened to the woman who looks for reasonable answers to these situations?" he teased, suddenly realizing that he wanted to take her in his arms and make soothing noises. She was putting on a good front, but the quaver in her voice was more revealing than she knew.

"Oh, she's right here," she said, moving closer and touching his arm. "But so is the girl who grew up on these stories. And if she gets a glimpse of floating lights or one little fireball, she's going to get downright hysterical!"

"I'll take care of her," Cody promised, wrapping an arm around her waist and tugging her closer still. As they approached the trailer, he leaned down and muttered, "But if she keeps on the way she's going, she's going to spook me, too."

Liann gave him a half smile and slid her arm around his waist, securing her thumb in one of his belt loops.

"Sammy!" Cody called as they neared the trailer. "Open up. It's Cody."

"Go away." The hoarse whisper, sounding like something out of a horror film, came from the open window above their heads.

Swearing softly, Cody tried the doorknob.

"Go away." The breathy whisper was softer, more desperate. "They're going to see you and come this way."

"Liann and I are the only ones out here, so open up."

"It's not people I'm worried about."

"Sammy," Cody said in a hard voice, "open the door."

"I tell you straight, Cody, I'm staying in here with the door locked until morning. So just—go—away!"

"Let me try," Liann whispered to Cody. At his nod, she said softly, "They're gone, Sammy. It's okay now."

"No, it isn't," came the stubborn whisper.

"How do you know?" she asked, pitching her voice even lower.

"Because of the drums," he said simply.

The hair on the back of Liann's neck stirred.

Cody felt her shiver and drew her closer. "There are no drums," he said, biting the words off impatiently, then looking down at her in concern.

A morose sigh drifted down from above. "I've been sitting here for an hour listening to them go thunk...thunk...thunk. They're not going away. And I'm not moving until they do."

"This is crazy," Cody muttered as another tremor worked its way down Liann's body. "Damn it, Sammy, open the door!"

"*Listen.*" The agitated hiss froze the two of them on the step. "There it is again. Thunk...thunk...thunk. They're not moving!" They heard a rustling sound from inside, and thought he was about to emerge, but they were wrong. Sammy cracked open the window a fraction wider, his whisper sharp in the warm air. "I tell you straight, Cody, they know I saw them and they're standing around deciding how to find me!" Then the window abruptly slid the other way until it closed with a snap.

Liann stared blankly up at the space where Sammy had been, then turned her gaze to Cody's face. It was a grim sight, she decided, wondering briefly why someone who didn't believe in spirits was taking the experience so much to heart. She wondered, that is, until he looked down at her, and then she had her answer. His hand slid beneath the fall of her brown hair and cupped her nape. Even in the dim light, she could tell that he was eyeing her anxiously, as if he expected her to break away and run screaming back to the car, demanding to be taken home. Of course, that's exactly what I'd like to do, she thought absently, as she toyed with a surprising notion. He was *worried* about her. Shoving the present crisis to the back of her mind, she considered the idea, and something warm and pleasant stirred deep within her.

She had been on the receiving end of a variety of emotions from him lately, ranging anywhere from disbelief to desire. The desire, she thought with deep feminine satisfaction, seemed to be cropping up on a regular basis these days. Even if she didn't want to deal with all the complications that Cody could bring to her life, desire in the abstract sense was a rather heady thing. And now, he was getting protective. Life, she decided with a small smile, was becoming very interesting.

While she had allowed her thoughts to drift, on some level she had been aware of Cody's warm hands sliding down her arms, his lips uttering soothing noises. Now his silence demanded her attention.

"I beg your pardon?" she said politely, hoping she hadn't heard what she thought she had.

"I said I guess we'd better go check this out," he repeated obligingly, confirming her worst fears.

Clearing her throat, she made a sweeping gesture with her hand and asked, "Out there?"

Cody nodded.

"It's dark," she informed him.

"I've got a couple of flashlights in the car."

He would, she thought bitterly. If he lived in California, he'd be the type to carry an emergency earthquake survival kit in the car, just in case the "Big One" struck while he was away from home. If he lived in Oklahoma, he'd make sure his place had a storm cellar. If he—

"Come on," he said, sliding his hand down to the small of her back and urging her off the step.

Liann reached out and grabbed his arm. "Wait a minute." She lifted one foot and waggled it, then pointed to her sarong. "I'm not exactly wearing ghost-chasing clothes."

Raising his brows, Cody grinned down at her. "Is there a dress code? But now that you mention it, will you tell me why on earth you wear those things?" He pointed to her medium-heeled thonged sandals. "They're nothing but scraps of leather."

"Because they're cute." She lifted her slim foot again and held it out for his inspection.

Cute. Cody looked down and wondered if there was a man alive who had ever worn something because it was cute. No, there wasn't, he decided, feeling as if he had just discovered something profound. But it was obviously only the tip of the iceberg, and interesting as the line of thought was, now was not the time to pursue it. Baffled, he shook his head. Cute.

"Come on," he said, stepping down and tightening his arm to bring her along with him. "Might as well get this over with."

"Cody," she protested, moving along beside him. "I mean it. I don't have the right kind of shoes for this."

He lengthened his stride and moved ahead of her. Opening the trunk, he reached in for the flashlight. "What kind of shoes do you need?"

Running shoes, she wanted to tell him. The kind that you tie to your feet so they can't fall off. The kind that have lots of bounce and traction. The kind that get you off to a fast start, that help you run marathons, that—

"We're just going to walk around and look," he said reasonably. "It won't take long."

Liann closed her eyes in resignation. He was like a runaway tractor. Nothing was going to stop him. Not her protests, not Sammy's conviction, not the dark, not even...the drumming of the marchers, she thought, catching her breath so sharply she almost choked. Over the faint noises Cody was making as he rummaged for the lights, another more ominous sound was stealthily flowing through the blackness.

Thunk...thunk...thunk.

"Cody," she said in a strangled whisper.

He muttered and moved a blanket out of the way. "I know they're in here."

Thunk...thunk...thunk.

"Cody." Liann felt her throat muscles tighten. Her lips were moving, but she wasn't making a sound. The rhythmic sound was merging with the beat of her blood, she realized dizzily, and she could no longer distinguish one from the other.

"Ah, here they are. They rolled over to the side."

THUNK...THUNK...THUNK.

"Cody." A faint thread of sound emerged this time.

He slammed the trunk and pointed toward the gate. "Let's start over there."

"Cody!"

He spun around as the almost imperceptible sound of her voice reached him. Later, she would think about how quickly he got to her, how secure she felt when he wrapped his arms around her, how the feel of his hard body almost drowned out the sound of the drums. Almost.

Thunk . . . thunk . . . thunk.

"What's the matter, honey?"

"What's the *matter?*" she hissed. "Are you deaf?"

"I hear your heart. Or do I feel it?" He drew her closer. "Let me see." One of his hands cupped her head, the other worked down her spine, coming to rest at the small of her back. He lowered his head, touching his lips to the corner of her mouth at the same time he applied pressure to her hips, bringing them home where they belonged.

Thunk . . . thunk . . . thunk.

Cody raised his head, muttering something Liann was just as glad she didn't understand. "What *is* that?" The words were deliberate, laced with annoyance.

"Drums?" she managed shakily.

Shaking his head in disgust, Cody said, "There's no drum on earth that sounds that way."

"I was afraid you'd say something like that," Liann said morosely. "How about an *un*earthly drum? A ghost drum."

Cody loosened his grip on her just enough to look down and examine the expression on her face. It was a combination of trepidation and hope. "Don't tell me Sammy has you spooked," he said finally.

Liann fought a battle between truth and the natural reluctance to appear foolish. Truth finally won. Partially. "A little, I guess."

He hauled her back against him to give her a hug. His chuckle was muffled in her hair. "I played the drums a bit in school. Believe me, honey, that noise can be any of a hundred things, but the one thing it *isn't* is a drum—real or supernatural. Come on, let's go find out what it is."

* * *

The drive home was done at a more sedate pace—and it was quieter. Grateful for the silence in the dark car, Liann decided that one of Cody's nicer qualities was that he didn't seem impelled to say, "I told you so."

How had it happened? she wondered again. What had triggered such an emotional response within her? She had spent years trying to separate fact from fiction. It was part of her job, for heaven's sake. Most of the papers and articles she'd written explained how present day superstitions had developed from early legends and myths. Maybe she ought to reread some of the stuff, she thought wryly.

"Feel better?" Cody asked quietly.

She could feel his gaze on her profile. He had sent several long, hard looks in her direction in the last few minutes. Probably wondering if she'd had her fill of mumbo jumbo for the night or if she was cooking up another hair-raising story for his entertainment, she told herself in disgust.

"If you must know, I'm feeling pretty silly."

"Why?"

He seemed honestly surprised, she realized with a surge of hope. Maybe she hadn't made an utter fool of herself after all. Suddenly that was very important, more important than she would have thought possible.

"I didn't want to go with you, you know," she admitted finally.

"I know."

She felt his smile and sighed. "I was more than half afraid that Sammy was right."

"I know." He reached out and took her hand, and his voice was as gentle as his touch. "That's why I admire your courage."

Liann straightened with a jerk. "Courage? You have to be kidding. I was the original Chicken Little. You were the cool one."

His grip tightened as she tried to withdraw her hand. "The gruesome sound of Sammy's whispering was enough to send anyone off—especially someone who...had reason to...be sympathetic to his story," he ended carefully.

"You're being very tactful all of a sudden," she said with a chuckle.

His grin was a flash of white in the dark. "I'm trying. I'm also trying to make a point."

"About what?"

"Courage. It didn't take any for me to start looking around. I expected to find pretty much what we eventually found."

"A group of people with flashlights looking for a lost set of keys?"

He nodded. "Something along that line. But you didn't know, and you went anyway." He raised her hand to his mouth and brushed its palm with his lips. "I'm impressed."

Liann wrapped her fingers around his and turned toward him as far as the seat belt would allow. "I tell you straight, Cody," she said in her best imitation of Sammy, "it was bad enough that you were right about the voices and lights, but when the drums turned out to be tennis shoes thunking around in a dryer, I was a little bent out of shape."

He grinned again, remembering the combined look of relief and disappointment on her face when they made the discovery. "Out here, sounds carry a long way," was all he said. "I wonder when Sammy will come out?"

"In the morning, I suppose. You saw how he acted. He wouldn't even open the window again when we got back." An unpleasant thought occurred to her then. "Cody," she said tentatively, "is this going to make any difference in the way you feel about having Sammy work there?"

He shook his head thoughtfully. "No. Even though he wasn't outside, he had everything locked up tight. I'll have a talk with him. Now," he changed the subject abruptly as he maneuvered the car into her parents' driveway, "what about you? Are you spending the night here?"

"No, I'll just pick up my car and go back to my apartment."

"Okay. I'll go in and say good-night and follow you home."

She looked up at him in surprise. "You don't have to do that."

Leaning over her, he released her seat belt and brushed her lips with his. "Yes, I do."

"I can take care of myself," she assured him. "I've been doing it for quite some time."

"Fine. Now you've got help. I take care of what's mine." And, as if that was supposed to settle the issue, he got out of the car and went around to open her door.

"I hate to break this to you, Cody," she said, ignoring his hand and glaring up at him, "but I don't belong to you."

"Maybe not yet," he agreed, dropping a hand on her shoulder and urging her toward the house. "But it's just a matter of time."

Chapter Four

Just a matter of time. The promise—or threat—followed Liann around like a persistent pup for the next few days, ambushing her in unwary moments and crowding in on her when she least expected it, whenever she looked up and found Cody's watchful gaze on her. It wasn't that he actually did anything, she thought after one of those moments. On the surface it was work as usual; not one word was said that she could object to. So why all of a sudden did she find herself empathizing with ancestors who had probably complained to the local *kahuna* about having a spell cast over them? she wondered fretfully. Probably because she was getting a firsthand lesson in the power of body language, she decided.

In the past, she had never given the subject too much thought. People moved, gestured and reacted—it was just a part of life. And now, it all seemed *larger* than life. Almost every move he made brought her head swiveling around in his direction, her breath catching somewhere deep within her. And he was deliberately crowding her, she thought with narrowing eyes. He was leaning on the corner of her desk as if he didn't have a perfectly good chair to sit on less than three feet away. When he did make use of it, his legs were stretched out, crossed at the ankles, so she all but fell over them each time she passed by. He reached out and touched her as he talked. In short, he was driving her insane.

Cody had delivered his message in no uncertain terms and had seemed to divest himself of a certain amount of tension in the process. Which was nice for him, she thought disgustedly, wishing she could say the same for herself. Unfortunately, his message had brought desire into the picture and the results were predictable: simple friendship had been banished and awareness filled the trailer. It left little room for the two of them.

That's it, she thought, sitting straighter. If she could convince him that the trailer wasn't big enough for them, that he needed to spread out more, she might start breathing on a regular basis again. As it was now, every time she stood up she seemed to brush against him. Every time she looked up from a book she looked right into his eyes. Sexual tension ricocheted off the walls like a living thing and rebounded between them. It made working conditions impossible, she told herself firmly. Surely he would see how reasonable she was being.

"Cody, I think this trailer is too—" she began. Then her brown eyes collided with his and her lips closed. The gleam in his eyes told her he already knew exactly where she was heading and that it was a lost cause.

"I ran into Herb Convers yesterday," he said in a casual voice. "He asked how we were doing here in the trailer and I told him that the setup was perfect."

"Did you, now?" Her voice was as bland as his. Mr. Convers was the head of the planning committee and her boss. Message received, she thought. Over and out. At least for now.

"Yeah." He leaned back and laced his fingers at the back of his head, his gaze holding hers. "My top priority is having you here when I need you. That outweighs the fact that things are a bit snug in here."

"Mmm," she murmured noncommittally. Blinking, she broke away from the intense communication of his gray eyes, allowing her gaze to drift down over the blue shirt that covered his muscular shoulders and wide expanse of chest. At his waist, a dark leather belt was threaded through the loops of jeans soft from repeated washings. Jeans that molded themselves to the long, lean muscles of an active man. A notch or two below his belt, her gaze was snagged again. Speaking of snug fits, she thought absently, suddenly aware of the straining fabric of his pants. "What?" she asked, blinking again and raising startled eyes to his face. *Guilty* eyes, she thought, furious with herself. "Sorry, I missed that."

"I said, what time are we due at Lily's?" he asked, watching with interest as a faint pink tinted her cheeks.

"Oh, uh, about one-thirty." Picking up a clipboard and heading blindly for the door, Liann told herself she was a fool, an absolute idiot.

Cody reached out and wrapped his fingers around her arm, just above the elbow. "Hold on," he said calmly. "It's almost noon. Let's get a bite to eat and head up there."

By the time they had a quick meal, Liann was almost back to normal. There was nothing like a hamburger and fries to shake off an attack of nerves, she decided, stretching like a sleek cat as Cody drove up the curving road. "Turn here," she murmured, reaching out and touching his arm. "Go *mauka* four blocks."

He slanted a quick glance down at her. "Want to try that in English?"

"Sorry," she said, a quick smile lighting her face. "Go inland. *Makai* is the other way, toward the sea. When you come to a dirt road, follow it all the way to the top." What could possibly go wrong on a day like this? she asked herself, shifting to a more comfortable position. The sun was shining, the sky was blue, the few clouds hanging around were puffy and white—just as it usually was on the leeward side of the island. All in all, it was a perfect day for visiting Tutu Lily.

She gave a quiet groan of contentment and answered her own question. Nothing could ruin such a perfect day. Nothing, that is, she amended cautiously after a moment's thought, unless Auntie Lily got on her high horse again, making impossible demands and telling Cody how to rebuild the Center. That would put a damper on anything. Of course, there was the possibility that she might go all mystic again. Remembering Cody's reaction in the office, the last time it had happened, a smile curved Liann's lips. As determined as he was to find logical explanations for all the things he was encountering, he was affected by the aura of power—for lack of a better word—that Lily emanated. He didn't want to be; in fact, he all but refused to be. But he was.

Power. That was precisely the word. Liann thoughtfully considered the older woman. Lily wore many masks, and even after all these years, Liann had not yet decided which was the true one. At times the old woman wore a mantle of dignity worthy of nobility, giving credence to the rumors that she was descended from the *alii*. At others, when she was thumping on doors and laying down the law, brash and ebullient, Liann didn't know *what* to think.

Then there were the times when Lily, speaking in a hushed, rhythmic cadence, seemed to be replaced by another, more formidable persona. A frown drew Liann's brows together. Those were the moments when she was overwhelmed by the magnetic force of the woman and believed for that brief span of time in unlimited power and unconditional authority—and wondered if this generously proportioned, many faceted woman held such power in her large hands. Then in a flash of an eye, the familiar Lily would return, leaving Liann with the disconcerting feeling that she'd missed something very obvious and important.

The first mask could possibly be written off as good breeding or fantastic stage presence. The second, she told herself, might be chalked up to eccentricity, but the third? Those were the moments of power that even a nonbeliever like Cody felt. And which mask was the true one? Perhaps all of them, she thought uneasily.

"You're frowning again," Cody said quietly.

"I do that frequently. I'm cultivating two sharp little character lines between my brows," she said lightly.

"You're puzzled about something. Or troubled."

Liann shook her head, even though she knew that the gesture wouldn't accomplish much. He was getting that look on his face again. The determined look. The I-want-to-know-what's-going-on-and-I-want-to-know-now look. The look that meant that he'd watch, and he'd wait, and he'd eventually wear her resistance down and drag it out of her.

"It's something to do with Lily, isn't it?"

"No," she said quickly, too quickly, hoping her recent efforts to improve her poker face had been successful. Obviously they hadn't, she decided after a quick look up at him.

"Liann, if you know something I should know, you'd better start talking. Fast."

"Look," she said, answering his grim tone as much as his words, "I don't. Honest." And that was the truth. She didn't know one blasted thing. Sure, she had questions and suspicions, but she had been on the receiving end of his raised-brow disbelief so many times, she wasn't about to comment on the preposterous scenario that was slowly taking form in her head. Maybe, she thought hopefully, if she took a couple of aspirins and slept for about twenty-four hours, it would go away. Or, if she was lucky, perhaps a nice, normal visit with Auntie Lily would dispel it.

Cody spent the remaining few minutes of the drive muttering about the condition of the winding red dirt road and directing a few suspicious glances at her.

"Lily doesn't want the road fixed up," Liann told him, wavering between sympathy and amusement. She herself expended absolutely no emotional energy on cars, merely expecting them to get her from point A to point B with the minimum of fuss, and the attachment men formed to their mechanical monsters never ceased to intrigue her. She pondered the enigma once again, watching Cody, who was the epitome of a strong, silent male, actually wince every time the BMW dipped into a rut. "She once told me that as long as it stays this way people won't be trampling all over her property."

"She's made a believer out of me," he grunted, flinching when a tire hit a large hole. "Once I get the car aligned, I won't be back in a hurry."

"Be brave," she said dryly, "it's just a few more feet. Pull in here." She pointed to where a grooved set of tracks meandered off to the right, "and park next to Lily's Blazer."

Cody killed the motor and stepped out of the car. He met Liann near the hood and draped an arm over her shoulders as he took in Lily's home with a quick professional glance. The small wooden house had obviously been constructed with durability in mind, but its simple design blended in pleasantly with the encroaching mass of trees, flowering shrubs and vines. The roof was thatched with the same fire-treated cane that had been used on Sean and Mei's house. The house was built on the highest point of the property, overlooking the lower hills and scattered homes below. Hoping that whoever had built the place had the good sense to allow for soil erosion, he headed for the front steps, urging Liann along beside him.

"Lily isn't here, but it's all right if we go in and wait."

When she didn't slow down, he held open the screen door. "How do you know?"

"Because she'd be out here on the porch rushing us inside," she said matter-of-factly, expanding on the first part of her comment. The latter part she considered obvious. "By the way," she added, preceding him through the door, "don't admire anything too much."

"Why not?"

The words had an absent ring to them, Liann noted, and she turned back to find that Cody had come to a dead stop in front of a magnificent wood carving of a bird in flight. "And don't, for heaven's sake, look at anything as covetously as you're looking at that!"

"Why not?" This time she had his full attention.

"Because native Hawaiians are the most generous people on earth. If you say you like something, it's yours."

"Just like that?"

She nodded, sympathizing with his startled expression. "Just like that. From then on, it's all downhill, a no-win situation. You feel rotten if you take it, your host is insulted if you don't. Take it from one who's been there, just play it cool."

"Aloha!"

The call came from outside, followed by a heavy tread on the front steps. Cody moved to the entryway and held open the screen door for Lily. She sailed through it just as he stepped aside.

She beamed at him. "You like my house, yeh?"

"It's very nice," he said noncommittally, wondering if Liann had been exaggerating, but unwilling to show more enthusiasm and risk having Lily sign the deed over to him.

"Come. I'll show you the rest of it." She led the way through the rooms that held her various treasures, pointing a sturdy finger at each one and saying, "You like it, yeh?"

The pieces she displayed were genuine works of art, paintings, bronzes, wood carvings, all of them focusing on the same bird.

"It is an *'io*," she explained, unconsciously caressing a bronze. "The Hawaiian hawk."

His fingers stroked the polished wood, his eyes lingered on them all, but he confined his comments to a tepid, "nice." Preceding Lily out of the last room,

Cody drew in a sharp breath. Straight ahead of him at the end of the hallway was a matted and framed photograph of startling beauty. It caught the savage elegance of the broad-winged *'io*, soaring gracefully in an updraft, silhouetted against the splendor of the setting sun. Walking slowly, his gaze never leaving the picture, he came to a halt in front of it.

"You like it, yeh?"

He nodded, grateful that she couldn't see his face, but he knew by the hesitant sound of her voice that he'd better dredge up an innocuous comment. Soon. It was either that or have her rip the thing off the wall and hand it to him.

"Auntie Lily?" Liann's voice broke the tense silence. "I was telling Cody about your view out in back. How you look down on the Institute. Do you mind if I take him out on the *lanai* and show him?" Without waiting for an answer, she reached out and took his hand, lacing her fingers through his and tugging him toward the kitchen.

"Look at this." Liann waved a hand at the one hundred eighty degree view as soon as they stepped outside on the wide, wraparound deck, which was adorned with a wall-to-wall collection of plants, vines and shrubs. "Have you ever seen anything like it?"

Lily's land was a prime piece of property that undoubtedly had developers salivating. That is, if they had ever risked their cars on the killer road to discover it. After assessing the area with a practiced eye, Cody was vaguely surprised to find that it was lower than he'd expected. The terrain's gently sloping surface gave way to a natural terraced look at one point, then resumed its gradual decline to the water. Several homes dotted the landscape at varying levels, and sprawled at the bottom was the Institute complex. Beyond that, the restless blue water was silvered by sunlight until it faded to a hazy mauve line at the horizon.

Lily moved up behind him. "Nice, yeh?"

Cody nodded in agreement, lulled by the contentment in her voice. "It's probably the closest I'll come to knowing what an eagle feels like in its aerie. There aren't even any trees in the way."

"Just the way I like it."

At first the silence seemed extraordinary, but gradually, sounds seeped through. First came the bird songs, the conversations and cries of the winged inhabitants. Then a shriek of child's laughter rose from one of the homes below. And from the Institute came the subdued rumble of earth movers, the ringing of a hammer on steel. Cody's eyes narrowed in a slight frown, knowing that if he owned this property, he would resent the intrusion of a huge domed building every bit as much as Lily did.

They were facing due west and Cody commented, "You must see some pretty spectacular sunsets."

Lily shrugged, a distant look on her face. "As you say. Soon I will miss them."

"Why? Are you moving?"

Turning her head to look straight into his eyes, Lily slowly shook her head. "I will stay forever on the land where I was born, where my father was born, and his fathers before him. They were here forever; I will be, too. But it will not be the same. You and the other city men will take away my sunsets."

A muscle flexed in Cody's cheek. "We're not stealing anything from you, Lily. We're simply putting up a building. Down there. It's over a mile away from your property."

"As the bird flies, much closer," she assured him.

She was right. Her view would never be the same. He didn't like it, but there wasn't one damn thing he could do about it. "It's legal," he reminded her.

She extended her hand and touched his shoulder briefly with one finger, and he had the feeling that she was trying to comfort him. "But not right, Cody Hunter. That is more bad reasoning." Straightening her arm, she pointed toward the water, a little to their right. "Today, and for the rest of the summer, the sun will set there. During the winter," she swung her arm several notches to the left, "it sets there."

Cody nodded, waiting for the other shoe to fall.

"But during the spring and fall," she pointed dead center between the other two points, directly over the proposed domed roof of the Center, "it sets right there."

With controlled precision, Cody brushed a leaf off the railing and waited.

But not for long. In seconds, Lily twisted the knife another notch. "For six months out of the year, I will see a building instead of sunsets." She let the silence work on her listener for a brief time. "Hawaiians have many ways that may seem strange to you." She waited for a moment and when he made no reply, went on. "For instance, we look to the sea for spiritual and physical strength."

Cody turned his head sharply.

Lily nodded somberly. "You are also taking some of that."

"Don't you think you're being a bit unreasonable? Look at all that water out there!"

"It has always been there," she said simply. "Now you are depriving me of part of something I have had forever." Turning abruptly, she said to the two of them, "Come walk with me and see my birds."

Several hours later, she watched as Cody closed the passenger door of the BMW and walked around to his side. "Laws rarely solve problems, Cody Hunter. People do that. Do you have a clear unwavering picture in your mind of what you want? In my picture, I see me standing on my *lanai* in six month's time, after the Center is complete. I look out over the water and I have the same view that I have now."

Cody flexed his shoulders, trying to brush away the tension that gnawed between them. "Lily, don't you see—"

She held up a hand, palm facing him. "You have a job to do, Cody Hunter. I have one, too. You have your way and I have mine. Perhaps we can learn from each other. When you awaken and before you sleep, close your eyes and see your picture." She slanted a quick glance at Liann, a curious smile curving her lips. "Possibly we will all get what we want." Turning, she walked to the house without a backward look.

Liann reached for her seat belt. Lily had had the final word again. Fussing unnecessarily with the belt, Liann wondered about that last look the older woman had given her. It had all the earmarks of a feminine *I know what YOU'RE thinking about, and it has nothing to do with a building*. Cody drove in silence, and grateful for whatever small blessings came her way, she noted that he was so preoccupied he forgot to flinch and swear when the tires fell into holes. He also didn't question Lily's final comment.

"Well, what do you think?" she finally ventured.

"I think that I have a clear unwavering picture of the Center being built exactly as it's planned," he said evenly, looking relieved when the tires slid back onto a blacktopped surface. "And I think she's going to be a disappointed lady, because this "picture" business isn't going to get her what she wants. She's not being realistic, and, as crazy as she makes me, I don't want to see her hurt. Can't you talk to her?"

"I doubt it. She believes in that as much as you do in the laws of physics. If I told you that domed roof was going to fall because I saw no visible means of support, would you listen?"

"Mmmm."

"That's what I thought."

Hours later, Cody lay flat on his back in his king-size bed and scowled at the ceiling. The bird lady was definitely getting to him. Almost every time he closed his eyes, he saw the outsized dome of the Center. It wasn't flattened the way Lily had once suggested, nor did it have slices cut out of it, as she had later recommended. It was a perfect ... white ... dome. It was also exactly where it was supposed to be, not shifted a millimeter to the right or left. The large front doors of the building were made of gleaming, red-grained *koa* wood and faced—what was it Liann said?—*mauka*, inland. With binoculars, he would probably be able to stand in the entryway and look straight up to Lily's deck.

He threw back the single sheet that covered his nude body, swearing softly at the blood thickening in his loins. Liann. All it took was a thought. Long before Lily had tried to brainwash him, he'd formed an image of Liann. A private, X-rated one. She stood facing him across the length of a large room—a bedroom. One small lamp softly illuminated a bed with a sheet and blanket pulled down, sheer curtains undulating in the breeze drifting through open sliding glass doors, and Liann.

She had on a silky white thing that lovingly hugged her body, its lower edge flirting around her ankles. With a small smile, she fingered a slim strap, and in tantalizing degrees, the cloth slid from her shoulders to rest on her small, high breasts. It clung to her beaded nipples for endless moments before dropping, catching and draping around the sweet flare of her hips. Finally, it slid one last time, pooling around her bare feet, and she opened her arms to him in an ageless gesture of feminine welcome.

Cody swung his legs over the edge of the bed. Swearing steadily, he strode to the bathroom and opened the shower door. With a savage flick of his wrist he turned on the cold water, stepped in and closed the door behind him.

Eleven short miles away, Liann dropped the book she was reading on the bed beside her. Even her favorite romance author wasn't going to do the job tonight, she decided in disgust. And turning out the light wouldn't solve a thing; sleep was definitely not on the agenda.

Darn Lily and her pictures. Of course, she admitted silently, she'd already developed her own very effective mental imagery before Lily had started tossing around instructions. And since the interior of the Center was her immediate concern, she didn't plan to waste any energy in a useless battle. Whatever happened on the outside of the building was going to happen, regardless of what she did or didn't do. So anything she imagined was going to be strictly on a personal level.

The problem was that she hadn't known that she had such a *good* imagination. Of course, Lily would say there was something wrong with her technique—a definite lack of concentration—because she couldn't seem to settle down to one picture. And maybe Lily was right. Her style was more in the nature of a collage. But what the heck, it was boring to concentrate on a single image when she could have a whole smorgasbord.

For instance, Cody standing with his back to her, legs spread aggressively, his hands jammed in his back pockets, the long, lean muscles of his back so inviting she could hardly keep her hands from running down them.

Or Cody's gray eyes on her, filled with lazy promise.

Cody saying, "I want you."

A bare-chested Cody, burnished hair arrowing down his chest.

Cody crowding her, a knowing look in his eyes when she moved away.

Cody tucking a strand of hair behind her ear, touching her cheek.

Cody touching her earlobe with a gentle finger.

Cody smiling down at her, a challenging gleam in his eyes.

Cody wrapping his lean hand around her arm, tugging her closer.

But the real killer was the latest image. Cody, wearing a towel knotted loosely at his waist, leaning in the doorway, watching every move she made, every breath she took. The games were over, his eyes promised. He padded softly across the thick carpeting and—

"No!" Liann said aloud, firmly putting her imagination in its place. She swung her legs over the side of the bed, got up and paced up and down the room, talking to herself. "Isn't one nasty lesson enough? Being a slow learner is one thing, but this is ridiculous!"

Del had given her enough trouble to last a lifetime, had put a dent in her self-esteem the size of Auntie Lily, and he was a pussycat compared to Cody! Was she crazy or what? Of course, Del hadn't done all of the damage by himself, Liann remembered; he'd had a willing accomplice in his bride. She'd had the strange notion that loving meant subjugating the person she was to become the woman he wanted her to be. And he had been immature enough to abuse the power she had given him.

Never again. She was a different person now, not nearly as trusting as she had once been. And that was all for the good, she told herself sturdily. She wouldn't even be tempted to get tangled up with an aggressive *haole* who would want to transplant her and turn her into Susie Homemaker. No, but she would be a bit self-indulgent and allow herself to lust over Cody Hunter. As long as it was done in the privacy of her own head, who was it hurting? And with that major decision behind her, she turned out the light and dropped down on the bed.

Half an hour later, she rolled over on her stomach and started counting birds. When she reached three hundred, she knew it was no use. She sat up with a martyred sigh, turned on the light and opened the book. If she remembered right, she'd left off with the heroine trying to convince the hero that a serious relationship was not in the cards. Thinking that she just might learn something helpful, Liann read far into the night.

Up on the hill, somewhere roughly between the location of Cody's apartment and Liann's condo, Lily prepared for bed. A satisfied smile curved her lips. She knew the power of the subconscious, had known it for years. She knew that whatever she imagined vividly enough, believed sincerely enough and acted upon enthusiastically enough, would surely come to pass.

Yes, she knew all that, but sometimes it was difficult to simply wait, to not participate more fully in the process. Sometimes she just had to do a bit more.

Chapter Five

Did your bookcase fall over?"

Liann looked up from where she sat on the living room floor, her legs crossed tailor fashion and surrounded by piles of books. She frowned and instinctively looked down. Her shorts were very pink and very short, not exactly what she wore when expecting company. Blinking, she tried to bring Cody into better focus. It wasn't an easy task because he stood on the other side of her front screen door, a dark silhouette with the morning sun at his back.

"Go away," she said pleasantly, lowering her gaze and reaching for another book while she tugged at the low neck of the equally pink knit shirt. "It's Saturday. I'm not on call. I don't have to soothe any ruffled feathers or defuse any emergencies until Monday." And I don't have to watch you prowl around, wondering when you're going to pounce, she finished silently. Opening the book, she turned to the middle section and faked an absorbed stare, listening for sounds of departure.

"*Did* your bookcase fall over?"

Liann looked up a second time and swallowed a groan. Cody had slid his hands into his back pockets and was slowly rolling his weight from his heels to the balls of his feet. He had the look of a man who had settled in for a long stay. "No," she told him, pointedly ignoring the fact that her greeting fell pathetically short of standard island courtesies. "What you see here is the result of a lot of work."

"You deliberately made that ... arrangement?"

Liann picked up on the not too subtle pause in his question. "What you really mean is this mess, don't you?" She waved casually at the teetering stacks of books almost encircling her, thinking of his neat desk. Cody was one of the most organized men she knew. Had ever known. There was never one unnecessary object on his desk. If he was looking at blueprints, there was a sheaf of blueprints on his desk. And that was all, aside from the telephone in the far corner. He was definitely a believer in the "a place for everything and everything in its place" doctrine.

She had occasionally caught his sidelong glances at her desk. They were composed of equal measures of stoic wonder and disbelief. In fact, she thought, he almost regarded her collection of notes, clipboards, books and general clutter with the same dislike he had shown on the road to Lily's house ten days ago. He never wanted to take his precious car on that washboard road again, and he probably dreamed about dumping most of her litter in the trash.

"Haven't you forgotten something?" he inquired gently, breaking into her thoughts.

She looked once again at the books scattered around the floor. She said vaguely, "I don't think so."

"You haven't asked me in."

Liann stared at him for a long moment. He wasn't going to give up, she decided with resignation. Apparently he was determined to pay her a visit and he wasn't going to be turned away.

"Won't you come in, Cody?"

There was still a remnant of a grin on his face at her excessively polite tone when he stepped in and closed the door behind him. His blue shorts and knit shirt were immaculate, Liann noted. They looked as if they had come from a ruthlessly organized closet instead of being snatched out of an untidy chest of drawers. They even had creases, for heaven's sake. He obviously didn't fiddle around with wash-and-wear stuff. White socks and running shoes covered his large feet.

Waving a hand at the sofa, she said, "Have a seat."

Instead, he moved a floral chair over until it faced her, stopping just long enough to take in her long, slender legs before he sat down. Nothing about her place surprised him, he decided after taking a long look around. She had exchanged the usual, generic off-white walls for a cool, subdued pastel. The cane furniture, with its boldly patterned cushions, was designed for comfort, and oiled oak tables and bookcases added a more substantial accent. Colorful framed prints hung on the walls and books were everywhere else. They overflowed the seven-foot cases, covered most of the flat surface in the room and were even used as door-stops.

"I like your yellow walls," he said blandly, his gaze returning to the point where her shorts brushed the tops of her thighs.

Her eyes narrowed in suspicion. "It wasn't easy getting that icy, sherbet effect," she said finally, opting to take his words at face value. "I almost drove the painters crazy."

"With a family the size of yours, you hired painters?"

She shook her head, a gleam of amusement in her brown eyes. "Nope. Blackmailed and called in old debts. Kai and some of the other guys did it. They got even, though. It practically cost as much to keep them in beer and food as it would have to hire someone."

Her hand strayed back to the tattered volume open in her lap, but before she could drop her gaze to the pages, Cody held out his hand. "That must be some book to keep you in here on a Saturday afternoon. Mind if I take a look?"

Liann hesitated, then with a small shrug, passed it to him. "Watch out, it's very old." Some of the tension left her when she saw how carefully he handled it, one large hand supporting the spine, the fingers of the other one slowly turning pages.

He looked at her questioningly. "*The Old Ways*?"

Easing her legs carefully between two stacks of books and stretching forward to relieve her back muscles, she said, "It's like an oral history. Stories taken down verbatim from some of the native Hawaiians. It's chockfull of wonderful stuff."

Wishing that she didn't sound quite so enthusiastic, he passed the book back to her. "Sounds interesting. Too bad."

"Too bad?"

"Yeah, because you might not want to tear yourself away from it."

"Why should I?"

"Because I came to see if you'd spend the rest of the weekend with me."

"The *weekend*?" Liann almost dropped the book.

"One day at a time, of course," he said calmly, leaning over to scoop it up before it hit the floor.

"Of course," she repeated, wondering if she looked as foolish as she felt. Someday, she told herself grimly, she was going to learn to think before she blurted out the first thing that popped into her head. "I don't know, Cody. I've really fallen behind in my work. I was going to spend these two days doing some catch-up stuff."

"I don't know of anything we're behind on."

Liann gave an exasperated sigh. "Not we, *me*. Did it ever occur to you that I already had a full-time job before you came along? I couldn't just drop everything when I started working with you."

For the second time in the few minutes that Cody had been in the room, she wished she had kept her mouth shut. If the expression on his face was any indication, his thoughts weren't ones she cared to hear. She had seen that flinty look on his face before, but it had never been directed at her. Now, she had the nasty feeling that, whatever her wishes, she was going to hear plenty.

"Are you telling me that you're trying to keep up with two jobs?" It wasn't really a question, more of an aggressive statement that he hoped, but didn't really believe, she'd refute.

Liann nodded, wishing more than ever that she'd never brought up the issue.

"And the times I've asked you to dinner, you've been working?"

She nodded again.

"Just what are you trying to prove?" Cody's voice had enough steel in it to make her wince. "Aren't eight hours a day enough for you? Are you out of your mind? How long do you think you can keep it up without falling flat on your face?"

Cody was on his feet, looking down at her and each question was coming harder and faster than the one before it. She didn't like anything about the situation, not his questions or his tone or his attitude.

"Just a darn minute," she said, getting up in one lithe movement and facing him. "My first job didn't end when you came along, you know. My own personal Simon Legree, better known to you as Herb Convers, asked me if I could juggle things around and try to keep the important things in the air. That's exactly what I'm doing, and I'm here to tell you, it isn't easy," she ended, marveling at her own bit of understatement. Back-breaking was a better word for it.

"Easy? It's impossible," he said flatly. "If you had any sense, you wouldn't even be trying. And, as of right now, you aren't."

"Stop...right...there, Mr. Hunter." Liann's words were distinct and encased in enough ice to slow him down. "If you think for one instant that you can give me orders, you'd better think again. You're not my boss, you don't sign my paycheck, and you don't have one ounce of authority over me. Is that quite clear?"

She held up her hand and plowed on before he could say anything. "I'm working with you because we all realized that an off-islander would probably need someone to run interference. We knew it would be inconvenient, but we all agreed that your work was so outstanding, it would be worth the effort. But remember this: I'm in that trailer every day as a courtesy. I am not one of your hired hands!'' She closed her eyes, drew a deep breath and exhaled sharply, stunned at the anger-induced adrenaline surging through her body. ''Do you want some iced tea?'' she asked a moment later, hoping that the topic had been thoroughly dealt with.

Cody nodded, watching in brooding silence as she turned and walked out of the room toward the kitchen, the sway of her hips distracting him. Then he winced as he heard the sound of ice crashing into glasses. If that meant what it sounded like, she was still as mad as a hornet. His gaze roamed around the room as he wondered what had set her off. What, besides his clumsy attempt to control her, that is. Obviously, he had touched a sore spot. And if he had to venture a guess, he thought, remembering the conclusion he had reached shortly after meeting her, it had something to do with an earlier bad experience. His comment by itself wouldn't have riled her so quickly. Yes, the lady had been badly burned and she was cautious enough not to get too close to the flame again.

Allowing a brief grin to slant the corners of his mouth, Cody sat back down. It didn't take a detective to figure out where she got her temper; one glance at her father's flaming hair was all that was needed. He had the feeling, though, that it didn't get the upper hand very often. No, Liann had been almost as surprised as he was, so it seemed that the lady with the dazzling smile kept her anger pushed so far down even she wasn't familiar with it. It was an intriguing combination, the gentleness and the fire. He wondered if she brought both of them to bed with her. He hoped so.

When Liann returned with the glasses and handed him one with a gesture that both of them recognized as a peace offering, she found him sprawled comfortably in the large chair with a thoughtful expression on his face. Resisting the impulse to tug at her shorts, she said, "I forgot to ask if you take sugar."

He shook his head. "This is fine."

She curled up in the corner of the couch and sipped her tea. In the few minutes she'd had to think it over, she realized her victory had come too easily. Cody wasn't one to walk off the field of battle without firing a shot. So she sat back, took a deep breath and waited. It wasn't long in coming.

"So why do you do it?" he asked mildly.

Liann blinked, both at the tone and the question. "Do what?"

"Try to juggle two jobs."

"Because I love what I'm doing." She responded so promptly that he knew she hadn't even thought about evading his question.

"What parts do you like best?"

"All of them, at different times. I never knew how much until—" She broke off abruptly and took a long swallow of tea.

"Until what?"

"Until . . . I was away from it for a while."

It was the way she said it that alerted Cody, the way she examined her drink, as if looking for an answer other than the one she gave. Matter-of-factly, he asked, "How long were you away?"

"Almost two years."

Two long, rough years by the sound of it.

"Why?"

In the next few seconds, he would either get an answer or he'd be out on his ear, Cody thought, his watchful gaze never leaving her. She would tell him it was none of his business or politely give the off-island lout the information he wanted.

"Because," she said finally, reluctantly, "I was married."

"And?"

"And I found out that my husband didn't like my job, my family, or anything that had to do with making me the person that I am. He talked me into moving to the mainland where he proceeded to mold me into a different person. Or at least he tried to," she added after a thoughtful pause. "I wasn't a very quick learner."

"Why did you stick it out for two years?" His voice was rough, probably rough enough to upset her, but all he could think about was having her ex-husband alone for a few minutes. It wasn't long, but what he had in mind wouldn't take long.

"I had some strange ideas about love," she told him, shaking her head slightly, as if she were discussing some anomaly that had happened light-years ago. "I thought I was supposed to do what I could to make him happy. It took me a while to realize that those things were supposed to be reciprocal."

"Did he . . . mistreat you?" he asked tightly, angered more by her throwaway statements than he would have been if she'd raged and cried.

"Oh, no. At least, not the way you mean. Things were just so sterile. He didn't want any of my books around, nothing that reminded him of my life here."

"So you left."

She nodded, summing up pain, failure and two lost years in three little words. "So I left."

"Good. What happened when you came home?"

Her lips curved at his brisk approval. What had happened? She'd faced the fact that Del had a big problem with possessiveness, then she filed for divorce and allowed her family members to offer comfort in various ways. And finally she'd learned to smile again.

In a voice devoid of emotion, she raised one finger and said, "I just picked up all the strings again." Except for forming relationships with men.

A second finger went up. "I got another job at the Institute." And worked like a slave to develop it into her present position.

A third one rose. "And now, things are pretty much as they were before." Except that she didn't trust as easily or as much.

Cody slowly flexed his shoulders, observing her controlled expression. Her restraint was the result of a hard-learned series of lessons, and he didn't like it any more than he did her colorless little statements. So she had "picked up the strings, got another job." What she meant was that her life had been turned upside down and she had managed, by the skin of her teeth, to hang on until things settled again.

He stood up and walked over to the window, keeping his back to her while he looked out past palm trees and the landscaped velvet green carpet, thinking about the man who had methodically drained the joy and laughter from her and knowing that a few minutes wouldn't do it after all. He hoped the cretin knew that he had failed; that he hadn't squeezed the life from her. That she had triumphed. And that he, Cody Hunter, was going to have everything that the mainland idiot had thrown away.

"Do you want some more tea?"

Cody turned from the window and reached for his glass. "Please," he said, hanging on to the tumbler, forcing her to lead the way to the kitchen so he could enjoy a closer look at her legs.

He expected to find the room cheerfully messy; it wasn't. Neither was the dining room. He mentally bet his week's paycheck that the rest of the house was equally tidy. So she wasn't a compulsive clutterer, after all. Interesting. Apparently it was only her books and work material that she needed spread around her like a large, paper security blanket.

Once they were back in the living room, Cody on one end of the sofa and Liann curled up on the other, he tried again. "These must be scattered around for a reason," he said, looking at the books.

Liann straightened defensively. "Of course they are. Do you think the place always looks like this?"

He waved away the implied accusation and leisurely examined the titles nearest him. "Since most of them deal with folklore, I imagine you're researching something."

"That's right."

"What?"

"It's a long story," she said, absently running her finger along the spine of the nearest book. "I doubt if you'd be interested."

"Let's get one thing straight between us, Liann," he said in a hard voice. "I'm not your ex-husband and I'm not threatened by your work. It's obviously a part of you and since I want to know more about you, I need to understand what you do and why you find it so rewarding. And when I ask a question, it's because I damn well want an answer."

Blinking in surprise, Liann wondered which was the more intimidating, his grim expression, his no-nonsense words or his hard voice. "I don't usually discuss this part of my work with people who don't . . ."

"Understand? Believe? How can I if you don't tell me about it?" he asked reasonably. Her lashes dropped, and he could no longer see her eyes. "So far, all I've heard about are spirits who walk in the dead of night and others who put hexes on things, and you have to admit that they're a little hard to take with no advance notice. On top of that, both times they were interfering with my work. Besides—"

"Okay, okay. I'll tell you about it, but if you get bored, stop me. I won't mind."

She would very definitely mind, but she'd never show it. It was obvious that she had learned to cope with rejection. She had a two-year degree in it. "Start with your job," he ordered.

Liann raised her brows at the command, then realized that he wasn't even aware of his tone. He was accustomed to giving orders and expected to have them followed. Stretching her legs on the cushions between them and crossing her ankles, she said, "My job. You asked earlier what I liked most about it. What I said was true, I do like it all. But I've spent most of my life listening to stories and folktales, so it's a real bonus to get paid to research myths and legends. To see if and how those stories still influence people today."

"What do you do with them when the research is done?"

"Write about them, usually. Sometimes for in-house publications, sometimes for local magazines. Somewhere down the road, when I collect enough of them, I may have a book. Who knows?"

"Is that your goal? To be published?"

She shook her head, saying, "Not really. As far as that goes, if you count the magazine articles, I already am. No, what I really want is to help my people preserve their cultural heritage, to see how things in the past might affect the present. I'm not the only one doing these things, of course. In the medical field, for instance, there are books already in print about native plants used as medicine in old Hawaii. It's exciting work, but it's not easy—especially these days."

"Why is that?"

"Because old people are the ones who have all of this information. And because their memories fade and they only remember fragments of things. You have to remember that none of this is written down. Things have been passed down orally from one generation to the next." She looked over at him with a smile. "And I get to travel around, talk to people, sift out the extraneous stuff and try to fit the proper pieces together."

Looking at her face, so vivid with excitement, and her eyes, which were wide with dreams, Cody almost felt sorry for the idiot who had been too blind to appreciate what he had. Almost, but not quite. Dismissing him with a blink, he reached out and wrapped his large hand around her crossed ankles, lifting them and settling them on his thigh.

"What are you working on now?" he asked when she stopped talking and eyed him uncertainly.

What am *I* working on? she wondered, as one of his fingers gently traced a line from her heel to the back of her knee. At the moment, she was definitely the one being worked on! Tentatively, she wiggled a foot and his hand slid back to her ankles. Giving him a severe glance, she tried to think about his question.

"I've been on the trail of a particular legend for a long time," she said slowly. "Most people think the story is complete as it is, but I don't."

"What's missing?" Cody asked, moving his hand to cup her instep, his thumb stroking her arch.

"That's the crazy part," she said, trying to ignore what he was doing and concentrate on what she was saying. "I don't know. I just have this vague feeling about it."

"Does it have anything to do with Lily?"

Liann stiffened and knew by the way his hand tightened on her foot that he felt it. "For heaven's sake," she managed in a fairly light tone, "why do you ask that?"

"Because every time we see her, you dive into a pile of books and mutter to yourself. And because, as usual, you're trying to lie and failing miserably."

"I don't think…maybe…I'm not really ready to talk about it right now."

"Why not?"

She tugged at her foot, but wasn't displeased when he tightened his warm hand around it, refusing to let go. "You've already said why. I've had to explain some stuff to you that sounds pretty preposterous, and you've looked at me like I'm a walking case of brain damage. My idea—and at this point it's pretty farfetched—would make the other things sound like run-of-the-mill bedtime stories."

"At least tell me the part everyone else knows."

She looked at him a long time. Finally she sighed and said, "Okay, but I'm warning you, I don't want any static about this. It's a simple story of how my people came to the Islands. One possible explanation, that is."

Leaning back and closing his eyes, Cody asked contentedly, "Does it begin the way all good stories do?"

"Of course," she said with a nod. "Once upon a time, when the world was young, my people, for whatever reason, had to leave their home. Some say that home was Tahiti, others say the Marquesas Islands.

"Where would they go? they asked each other. Where would they find the valley of rainbows, the heart of their dreams? They weren't sure, but they began to prepare for a long journey. Each person in the village helped make new lashings and sails for the three double-hulled canoes. The high priest and king retreated to the temple, communicating with the gods and reading all omens. As trees were hollowed and the boats took shape, the king slept several nights in each one, sharing his *mana*, the power he got from nature, so that the canoes would be strong and courageous. And each night he prayed that a dream would guide him.

"Others who prayed for guidance were the navigators. It would be their responsibility to find the new land. They had no instruments to determine longitude and latitude, but they knew which stars stood over each island. They had learned as boys, listening to the chants that their fathers had learned from all of the fathers who came before them. One such chant gave obscure directions to a new land in the north.

"Perhaps, they thought, the birds knew of this land. For did they not flock together when the sun made its trip to the north? Did they not fly over the ocean, beyond the horizon, over waters untouched by man? There must be land, the men argued, for the birds could not sleep on water. And yet, months later, they would return with the sun. Then one night, in a dream, a navigator stood on the shore watching the birds depart on their long journey. When they were mere specks in the sky, one bird separated from the flock and flew back to the man. It landed on his shoulder and whispered into his ear, 'To find the land you are looking for, follow our path.'

"And that is what the brave people did. They finished making the boats and took them into the open sea to test them. Provisions were assembled, tabus were imposed, seeds and plants were carefully wrapped, and with one final ceremony, the ships were launched.

"The progress was measured at night by the stars. During the day, the navigators made note of such things as how the ships moved in the waves, how the spume rose, and the ever-changing color of the sea. They tasted the water and looked for temperature changes. At all times, they heeded the motion of the ground swells, the long waves which march across the ocean floor.

"After many days, the people were exhausted, hungry and thirsty. They had survived angry storms that frightened them and made them wonder if they misread the omens. Their food was almost gone; there was only enough water for a few swallows a day.

"When despair began to eat at their hearts, the gods heard their prayers. They sent a bird with a message of comfort. It flew over the ships, heading due north, saying, 'Follow me. Follow me home.' And as surely as they had known for so many days that no land was within sight, the navigators *knew* that their new home was just over the horizon.

"The men dipped their paddles into the water with renewed strength, the women brought them what little food was left. Burning, painful muscles were forgotten as a hazy shape formed where the water met the sky. They paddled through the night, and with the rising sun came the sweet, sharp fragrance of land. Clouds lifted and their voices rose in praise as they saw the vast island before them. Cliffs loomed ahead and they paddled faster yet, past waterfalls and jagged shorelines of black rock. Ahead of them, the green mountains were adorned in sunlight, raindrops and an arc of bright, pure colors.

"They paddled into a small lagoon, chanting reverently to their gods as a large valley opened before them. They had found their valley of rainbows, the heart of their dreams."

Chapter Six

"I see now why you're so good at your job," Cody said quietly, looking at her. "If you write the way you tell the story, someday you're going to have a best-seller on your hands."

Liann wiggled her feet and he loosened his grasp. Swinging her legs to the side, she stood up and said, "I don't know about that. Right now, the fun is in the learning. And...I care." She moved restlessly and changed the subject. "Give me a few minutes to change, and we'll go out and join the tourists. But I warn you, if you go with me, you'll see my island as I see it. You won't be coming back with an armload of souvenirs."

"Promise?"

She stopped in the hallway, looking over her shoulder. "Promise."

"Thank God."

Listening to her soft laugh, he thought about what she had said. Yes, she cared. More than that. Some part of her actually seemed to live in the past, feeling what those early people had felt. His mind drifted to what she had told him earlier. He was still thinking about her two years of exile and how they must have affected her when she returned, stuffing things into a tote bag. Sterile was the word she'd used to describe them, he thought grimly, getting to his feet. Another understatement if he ever heard one. Mildly surprised at the residue of anger still burning his stomach, he looked at the glowing woman before him and found it hard to believe that she had ever been unhappy.

Her red print blouse was tied at her midriff. The hem of the matching skirt flirted around her knees, showing off her long, slim legs. She caught him contemplating her shoes, which were little more than cork soles and white straps, and grinned. She had pulled her hair to one side and caught it in a braid that fell over one shoulder and rested between her breasts.

"I'll be ready as soon as I find my purse. Ah, there it is." She bent over the back of a chair and lifted it from behind several books. When she straightened and turned around, the look on Cody's face froze her where she stood. She was neither naive nor stupid enough to ask what was the matter. She knew. He wanted her. At that moment, he was the embodiment of all that his name implied: a hunter. Taut and still, he emanated enough danger signals to shift her instincts into an uproar. They urged her to move, run, get out of his way. But one quiet voice told her to be still.

Then, just as quickly as it had come, it was over. Everything about him softened, the set of his jaw and shoulders, the tension in his body, the gleam in his gray eyes. Everything. Liann took a deep, slightly shaky breath, and dug her keys, wallet and lipstick out of her purse. The latter two were dropped into her tote bag; she held on to the keys until she locked the door. A few minutes later, Cody held the car door open while she got in.

He slid in beneath the wheel while she was still fiddling with the seat belt. Nodding in the direction of the building complex, he asked, "Don't you find it confining to live in a place like that? Especially after growing up in your parents' home?"

Leaning back against the seat as he pulled out of the parking lot, she thought about her answer. "No, I don't see it that way. It's attractive and clean, the people are friendly and there's as much togetherness as a person wants. Every evening, for instance, we gather for a drink and watch the sunset."

"We?"

"If that's what I want. If not, then it's *they*. I also have as much privacy as I want, so I have the best of both worlds. It's fine for now. Besides," she began, then hesitated, wondering why she was searching so hard for an honest answer. Probably because if he didn't get one, he'd keep nagging until he did, she told herself dryly. "Besides," she repeated in a firmer voice, "it was time for me to move, to be on my own."

"Did you go back to your folks' place while you got your divorce?"

"For a while," she said shortly, looking straight ahead.

Cody changed the subject abruptly. "Which way should I go?"

"Turn up here at Kuakini Highway and head south. I'll tell you when to stop."

"Do I get to know where we're going?"

Liann shook her head. "Nope. I want you to be surprised."

Less than an hour later, he decided that he was. The last thing he had expected her to do was take him to a national park. He told her as much when they left the car and headed toward the entrance. "I expected something different."

"Different in what way?"

"Older, I guess."

Smiling, she pointed to a newspaper article taped to the window of the ranger's office and stood quietly while he read it. Her gaze remained on his face and she wished she knew what he was thinking. The article began with a short warning: Do not take lava rock away from Hawaii; it will bring you bad luck. Then it presented case after case of tourists who had taken various-sized chunks home with them, met with accidents and an assortment of catastrophes and finally mailed the lava rocks back to the island, hoping to break the dark spell under which they found themselves.

Cody took off his sunglasses and looked down at her, then indicated the newspaper. "Do you believe this?"

She gave him the smile he was getting used to. The one that was accompanied by a little shrug. The one that said, *beats me*. "I'd like to say no," she assured him. "And I can't bring myself to give you an unequivocal yes. All I can tell you is, I would *never* take lava off this island." Giving a small laugh at his groan, she hooked her arm through his and said, "Come on. You want old, I'll give you old."

They walked through a tall wooden gate into another world.

"It doesn't matter how often I come here, it never fails to take my breath away," Liann said softly.

A small, impossibly beautiful lagoon lined with tall palms curved before them. A wooden canoe was beached well beyond the reach of the vivid blue water. Palm fronds whispered in the breeze and water lapping on the sand were the only sounds that broke the silence.

"The Garden of Eden?" Cody asked in a lowered voice.

"Almost. The Place of Refuge, established during the early fifteenth century." Nudging him forward, she nodded at a sturdy stone platform. "This supported a temple at one time."

Cody glanced around, taking in the various artifacts and replicas of ancient buildings. "Refuge from what?" he asked.

"This sanctuary," Liann said, waving a hand to encompass the entire area, "was the poor man's answer to the *kapu*, the law. In a time when the social system was one of feudalism, the poor man needed all the help he could get. There was a rigid class distinction that was reflected by the *kapus*. The king was at the top of the heap and he could hardly do any wrong; the common man was at the bottom, and it was easier to get in trouble than to stay out of it."

"What kind of trouble?"

"You name it, he was in it," she said as they moved toward a line of tall palms. "*Kapu* was what the law was called, but it actually means taboo, forbidden. And to the common man, almost everything was forbidden." She looked up at him, her face alight with enthusiasm as she warmed to her subject. "Although this place is also called the City of Refuge, it was never a city at all, at least not one that had permanent residents.

FREE BOOKS!

FREE GIFTS!

PLAY THE "LUCKY 7" SLOT MACHINE GAME!

AND YOU COULD GET FREE BOOKS, AND SURPRISE GIFTS!

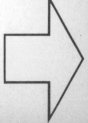

NO COST! NO OBLIGATION!
NO PURCHASE NECESSARY!

PLAY "LUCKY 7"
AND GET AS MANY AS SIX FREE GIFTS...

HOW TO PLAY:

1. With a coin, carefully scratch off the three silver boxes at the right. This makes you eligible to receive one or more free books, and possibly other gifts, depending on what is revealed beneath the scratch-off area.

2. You'll receive brand-new Silhouette Romance® novels, never before published. When you return this card, we'll send you the books and gifts you qualify for *absolutely free!*

3. And, a month later, we'll send you 6 additional novels to read and enjoy. If you decide to keep them, you'll pay only $1.95 per book. And $1.95 per book is all you pay. There is no charge for shipping and handling. There are no hidden extras.

4. We'll also send you additional free gifts from time to time, as well as our newsletter.

5. You must be completely satisfied, or you may return a shipment of books and cancel at any time.

This may be your lucky play...
FREE BOOKS and FREE GIFTS???
Scratch off the three silver boxes
and mail us your card today!

PLAY "LUCKY 7"

Just scratch off the three silver boxes with a coin.
Then check below to see which gifts you get.

YES! I have scratched off the silver boxes. Please send me all the gifts for which I qualify. I understand I am under no obligation to purchase any books, as explained on the opposite page.

215 CIL HAXX

NAME

ADDRESS   APT

CITY   STATE   ZIP

7	7	7	WORTH FOUR FREE BOOKS, FREE SURPRISE GIFT AND MYSTERY BONUS
🍒	🍒	🍒	WORTH FOUR FREE BOOKS AND FREE SURPRISE GIFT
⬤	⬤	⬤	WORTH FOUR FREE BOOKS
🔔	🔔	🍒	WORTH TWO FREE BOOKS

Terms and prices subject to change.
Offer limited to one per household and not valid for present subscribers.
PRINTED IN U.S.A.

"Except for a few *kahunas*, the population was strictly transient, an endless stream of fugitives seeking forgiveness for violating *kapus*. Only the foolhardy deliberately broke one, because the result was instant death. But the system consisted of so many 'dos' and 'don'ts' that it was impossible for everyone to remember, much less observe, them all."

Cody draped his arm around her shoulder, matching his stride to her shorter one. "Specifics, Liann. What sort of *kapus* did they break?"

"Patience. I'm trying to give you the background." She deciphered the long-suffering gleam in his eye and grinned. "A man could be killed for eating with women or eating food cooked by women, for touching the king, his garment or shadow, even for stepping unknowingly on the chief's footprint hidden in the grass. It was bad news to be on the losing side in a battle, and he had to watch out for defilement by women."

"Were the women exempt?"

"From *kapus*?"

He nodded.

"No," she said cheerfully. "They were definitely second-class citizens. Men came from the light, women from the dark, men were clean and women impure. The list is endless. Women couldn't eat pigs, coconuts, certain fish and the banana." At his questioning look, she explained. "The banana was created by the gods to represent man's fertility. Women were also locked up in tiny rooms on certain days of the month, when they were considered most impure. I hope that none of them were claustrophobic, because it meant instant death if they tried to escape."

"And all they had to do to be pardoned was to come here?"

"They had to *get* here," she told him, emphasizing the difference. "And that wasn't easy. Usually the king's soldiers were right on their heels, waving clubs and spears. Of course," she said thoughtfully, "there was the water. If they made it to that point," she turned and indicated a spit of land to the north of the refuge, separated from it by a deep bay, "they could swim. That in itself wouldn't have been much of a challenge for an islander, but see that dark patch of water out in the bay?"

"That one?"

She nodded. "It's called Lua Mano, den of the shark."

"If and when they got here," he said with exaggerated patience, "what happened?"

"That was the good part. They were purified by a *kahuna*, usually within a day. Then they could leave and no one could touch them. If they were refugees from a war, they just waited for peace, and had the same immunity. Nice, huh?"

"For the ones who made it," he said dryly.

"Just imagine a beautiful young lady who has ferocious temper tantrums," Liann said.

They were standing on an observation point in Volcanoes National Park, overlooking the steaming Kilauea caldera. Sulfurous fumes permeated the entire area.

"I can see it coming," Cody said, reaching for her hand. "You're going to give me a nice, scientific explanation of volcanoes."

Liann nodded serenely. "This young woman, when angry, stamps her foot on the ground. After it trembles with earthquakes, cracks appear in the earth, and she commands torrents of molten lava to run down on those who have angered her. That's Madame Pele, Goddess of Volcanoes. Legend pictures her as a lady with restless feet, and that's exactly what she is. She rages in one place, then withdraws and sulks for a while before showing up somewhere else and kicking up a fuss. That's the general picture found in ancient Hawaiian mythology.''

"And she's still alive and well?''

After pointing silently at the steam rising from the crater, Liann raised her brows. "What do you think?''

Cody looked and finally said, "I think she seems a bit spiteful.''

"Capricious might be a better description. And spoiled. The early Hawaiians knew better than to fool or defy her because her retribution was fast and disastrous.''

"And what did they do to keep her off their backs?''

"First of all,'' she warned, "they were respectful. One thing they learned early on was that the *ohelo* berry, which grows around here because this is her home territory, is a favorite of hers. It's one of Pele's sacred plants. In order to avoid bad luck, when eating the *ohelo* berry, smart people first offer a few to Pele by tossing them in the direction of her home.''

"Anything else?''

"Of course.'' She turned away from him, looking determinedly down at the black-and-gray basin. "When she takes human form—''

"I knew it!''

"—those who have seen her described her as a young, beautiful woman with flowing hair, which can either be blond, black, or when she's angry, red. But just as often, she's been seen as an old lady. Either young or old, she usually had a small dog with her.

"I've heard hundreds of stories told by island people, as well as mainlanders, who say that they were driving down a road and saw a woman walking or standing by the side of the road. Those who didn't want to risk her anger by not offering her a ride would stop. She would get in without saying a word and disappear before they arrived at their destination. Those who didn't offer her a ride would inevitably have some sort of car trouble along the way."

"What do you think this is, Disneyland? No, I don't have any Sleeping Beauty stories," Liann said as they left the volcanoes and drove down the winding road toward Kaimu. "But I can give you the dwarfs without Snow White," she added thoughtfully, a smile curving her lips when he winced.

Cody groaned, amusement gleaming in his eyes. "You're really going to do it, aren't you? Dwarfs."

"Wasn't it the Greeks who used to warn people to be careful what they asked for?"

"Probably. They were full of good advice. I should have listened."

Liann suddenly realized how much she was enjoying herself. The hours had sped by, eased no doubt by the fact that Cody had turned off his massive aura of sensuality. Or rather, dimmed it considerably. It had been in evidence just enough to make her feel very feminine, and to appreciate the fact that she felt that way. It also, she thought with a sense of shock, had worked its way through the buffer zone she kept between herself and most men. And she had a nasty feeling that Cody had intended things to work out exactly that way.

"Dwarfs," she said determinedly, deciding to think about it later. "There are a number of theories as to when and how the island of Kauai was first inhabited."

"By dwarfs."

"You're really going to have to do something about your impatience, Cody. I'm getting to them. There are some popular fables about the *menehune*, supposedly a group of lower-class Polynesian people. Modern legend describes them as a race of little people, somewhat like leprechauns."

"I can't stand this."

"They were rarely seen, and worked only at night. In one night, they would complete an amazing amount of work and would accept only a single shrimp per worker as payment."

"Someone should have informed the labor board."

"One of the many construction projects attributed to them is the Menehune Ditch in Waimea."

His face turned to her for a second. "Are you serious?"

"Being in the construction business yourself," she said blandly, "you should really make it a point to visit it. Supposedly it indicates a knowledge of stonework not seen anywhere else on the islands. Of course, I'm no judge of such things, but you might—"

"You win. I'll go if you'll come along and show me where it is."

"It's a date."

"Let's get out here and walk for a while," Liann suggested.

Cody eased the car over, pulled to a stop between two palm trees and turned off the key in the ignition.

"We're in luck today," she said, after looking around. "We've got the place to ourselves. No blasting radios, barking dogs or flying balls. It's the only way to enjoy your first visit to the black sand beaches. Come on, let's get out." Impatiently, she opened the door, stepped out, kicked off her shoes and placed them on the floor of the car. Digging in her tote bag, she pulled out a towel.

Cody took off his shoes and socks and walked around to her side just as she undid the button at the waist of her skirt. He watched with silent appreciation as she unwound the material. "Nice shorts," he said, lifting his gaze from her tanned legs.

"Thanks." With a smile, she reached up and draped the towel around his neck. "Let's go test the water." She met his outstretched hand with hers, lacing her fingers through his before she turned and led him to the shade of the tall, slender coconut palms. In places, the frothy water lapped around the trunks of the trees. Stopping to look up, she said softly, "When I was a child, I used to think the swaying trees were dancing to the music of the wind."

As they walked along the coarsely textured, wet, black sand, with the water alternately washing over their ankles and receding, Cody dropped her hand and draped his arm around her shoulders, tugging her closer. Liann pulled her arm out from between them and wrapped it around his waist.

He was a comfortable man to be with. The thought, coming from out of nowhere, surprised her. He was also annoying, sexy and disturbing, she reminded herself as she lengthened her stride, trying to match his. But she didn't have to talk like a windup doll when she was with him or feel that he had to be entertained.

Cody's gaze seemed to measure the contrast between the black sand and the creamy waves, between the green palm fronds and the blue sky. "It's beautiful here."

"Yes."

Something in her voice caught his attention and he looked down at her, trying to read the fleeting, vaguely unsettled expression in her eyes. "Why do you say it that way?"

"What way?"

"With regret," he said slowly, as if groping for the right word.

She waved her hand, encompassing all that was around them. "Because it's slowly disappearing, and I hate to think that anything this lovely won't be around forever."

"Disappearing?"

Turning to look back at the slender trees so near the water, she said, "At the turn of the century, those were a quarter of a mile inland. A lot of them have already toppled. The waves and the tides are always pulling at the sand, taking it out and dropping it at the base of the underwater cliffs."

When his arm tightened around her, offering comfort, she blinked and said, "I don't know why I'm going on like this. It's here today, and that's what's important."

"I'm disappointed," Cody said abruptly.

Liann looked up, surprise deepening the brown of her eyes. "Why?"

"I haven't heard one ghost story. I thought you were setting me up for a drowned *kahuna* or something."

A sudden grin curved her lips. "Would I do such a thing?" She blinked, surprised again by the look of satisfaction on his face.

One large hand wrapped around her nape, and a warm thumb tilted her chin so that he could kiss the tip of her nose. "I don't even think I'd mind. I'm getting used to it."

Trying to ignore the sudden pounding of her pulse, Liann backed away and said briskly, "We've got a long drive ahead of us, I think we should start back."

Cody looked down at the brown eyes so busily evading his and wondered what had spooked her. She was a mass of contradictions, one minute teasing and leaning against him, the next as skittery as a cat in the rain. But that was just about what he'd expected, he thought, taking another look as she turned back and dipped a foot in the water. Nothing about her was proving to be simple. Which meant he just had to work harder. If he intended to break down the barriers she kept erecting between them, and he did, he obviously had to get a handle on something that had never been his long suit: patience.

"How do you feel about coming to my place for a barbecue tonight?" he asked. "We can stop at the next decent store and pick up some stuff and avoid the crowds in Kona."

"Can you cook?" she asked with interest.

"As long as it's done outside on a grill. Can you make a salad?"

"I'll give it my best shot."

"Good. Let's get going." He reached for her hand.

"Wait a minute. Rinse your feet in the water and dry them off."

"Why? They'll just get dirty going back to the car. Let's do it there."

"Trust me, Cody. They won't. Do it my way." When he looked as if he was going to be stubborn about the whole thing, she sighed and said, "Why do you think I brought the towel? Black sand is different from your run-of-the-mill sand. It comes from the lava and it doesn't cling and stick like the other kind. And I don't know why," she said in a rush before he could ask. "So don't argue, just do it!"

As they drove away, he said, "I hate to admit it, but you were right. If we could just figure out what to do with the stuff, we could make a fortune."

"And probably walk right into a hornet's nest. I think Madame Pele has a patent on it."

"You didn't want me to take this road, did you?" Cody shot a quick glance at Liann's tense profile. She was staring straight ahead and, judging from the deep line between her brows, her thoughts weren't pleasant.

"No, not really."

"It'll save us a lot of time."

"I know."

"It's a decent road."

"I know."

"A little rough in spots," he admitted, "but okay."

"Ummm."

"It was the logical choice."

"Uh-huh."

"So what's the matter?"

"Nothing."

"Liann." There was a warning note in his voice.

"It's okay."

"The coastal route would be almost twice as long."

"I know."

"The map clearly shows that this road practically cuts the island in half."

"I *know*, Cody."

"So give me one good, logical reason why we shouldn't be here."

Blast the man, she thought fretfully. He still talked about logic. By now, you'd think he'd realize that reason didn't have much to do with what went on around here. Saddle Road wasn't a place where people stopped to talk about logic. It was a road that cut through the heart of the island, one that people traveled as quickly as possible. It was a road where unreasonable, unexplainable things occurred. It was definitely not the place to be after sunset, when the dark loomed around them in threatening, pouncing shadows.

Of course, she had never personally experienced anything, she reminded herself. But, she had never pushed things to the limit and traveled the road at night, either.

"There aren't any emergency phones along the road," she offered feebly.

"So?"

"What if something happens to the car?"

Cody patted the steering wheel as if it were alive. "Nothing will. It's the most reliable car I've ever had."

"Do you have plenty of gas?"

"I filled the tank before we left the store, remember?"

"Oh, yeah."

Cody reached out and took her hand in his. "You're cold." He pressed her hand against his thigh, covering it with his. "Are you nervous?" he asked, a tinge of surprise coloring his voice.

"No!" she said quickly. Too quickly.

"You are." His hand tightened on hers. "Honey," he said comfortingly, "if anything *does* happen, I'll take care of you."

Easy for him to say, she thought morosely. Height and bulging biceps might intimidate a stray mugger or two, but they'd have absolutely no impact on the things that hovered over Saddle Road, especially after dusk.

As if she had conjured up something out of the darkness, the smooth hum of the motor shifted key, hesitated, then resumed its powerful hymn of strength and reliability. Cody's body tensed and relaxed in rhythm with the car.

Five minutes later, the motor coughed and died. Cody swore and maneuvered the car over to the side of the road. He got out, grabbed his flashlight and looked under the hood while Liann gave herself a pep talk.

It's just something simple, she assured herself, refusing to look out the window at the encroaching darkness. He'll fix it and we'll be on our way. She maintained the litany while Cody tinkered and muttered some highly inventive oaths. There was absolutely no reason on earth for her to mention the unusual...happenings credited to this particular stretch of land. It was the car, pure and simple. Besides, one more story on top of those she had told him during the day might just well be the proverbial straw. No, it had to be the car.

Cody slid behind the wheel and tried the motor. "Damn!" He got back out and tinkered some more. When he returned and tried again, it wasn't any better. He sighed sharply and turned to Liann. "I'm sorry, honey. It looks like we're stuck. We'll just have to wait until someone comes along."

They sat in silence. Cody seemed to be mentally reviewing the car's innards, wondering if there was something he had missed. Liann occupied herself by thinking of their day, beginning with Cody's surprise appearance and ending with their hurried shopping in the grocery store. They had separated, each selecting their own ingredients, then she had browsed at the magazine rack while he paid the cashier.

She stiffened as an awful thought crossed her mind. "Cody," she said tentatively.

"Hmmm?"

"What kind of meat did you buy?"

"What?"

"The grocery store? Meat? What kind did you buy?"

"Ribs," he said in an abstracted tone, his mind obviously still beneath the hood of the car.

"Pork or beef?" she asked in a voice of doom, knowing full well what he was going to say.

"Pork."

"Throw it out."

Cody jerked around and stared at her as if she had lost all sense of reason. "What?"

"Throw it out. Now."

"No."

A sensible person wouldn't have argued with that flat refusal, but Liann wasn't feeling sensible. "Cody," she said between gritted teeth and leaving little spaces between each word, "Pork is bad luck on this road. If you want to get out of this godforsaken place, throw the damned stuff out. Now."

Sighing in frustration, and clearly determined not to make a bad situation worse by arguing, he reached behind him and rummaged through a brown paper sack. He hefted a cold mound wrapped in white paper, then heaved it out the window.

"Now start the car," she said quietly.

He gave her a long, level look, then turned the key in the ignition. The powerful motor caught on the first try. Neither of them said a word as the car accelerated and sped down the winding road.

Chapter Seven

There," Cody said, driving in one last finishing nail.
"Will that do?"

Liann swiveled around in her desk chair and looked,
but at Cody rather than the project he had just com-
pleted. He had his back to her and her lingering gaze
drifted down from his muscular shoulders, over the lean
stretch of his back and on to where the leather belt
threaded through the loops of his khaki pants. The
creases on his tapered shirt had the same military precision they had had hours earlier when he'd begun.

Taking a quick look at the finished product, her eyes
widened in appreciation. "You know it will. They look
wonderful. Thank you. But I don't think you should
have done it," she said, her protest a sop to her receding conscience. She coveted the bookcases too much to
be sincere, and it had been obvious right from the start
that even if she had kicked up a royal fuss, it wouldn't

have made a whit of difference. Cody had decided that
she needed bookcases, and bookcases she would have.

He ran a hand over the wood grain, absently testing
for rough spots. "I should have thought of it sooner."

"Why?"

He looked over at her desk, at the teetering piles of
books that encroached on her work space more each
day. "If I had used my eyes, I would have noticed that
you were getting a little crowded over there."

"You didn't know I needed all this reference material," she said fairly, absolving him of blame. "How
could you? You didn't even know I was trying to keep
up with all of my other work."

A muscle in his jaw tightened. "No, I didn't, did I?"

Having been through that scene once and not wanting to repeat it, she hurriedly asked, "Are you sure that
there's nothing you want me to do? I've been spending
a lot of time on my research this last week." And we
both know why, she thought, as he turned back to the
case and poured oil on a clean cloth.

He didn't look around, just began polishing the dry
wood with long, even strokes, his muscles moving
smoothly beneath the blue shirt. "Feeling guilty?"

"A bit." It had been nine days since he'd learned
about her sixty-five hour workweeks. Nine days since
he'd thrown the pork out of the car on Saddle Road.
And although they had been together every day, not
once had he mentioned either occasion.

"Don't. You deserve a break, and things seem to be
settling down. No more suspicious bones have turned
up. Sammy says everything is quiet at night and Lily has
apparently accepted the inevitable. At least, she hasn't
been around while I've been here. Have you seen her?"

She shook her head. "Not since we went up there. She called once, checking to see if we were making 'good pictures,' but I told you about that."

"Yeah." With a minimum of fuss, he capped the oil bottle and wiped the wood one last time with a clean cloth. Stepping over to her desk, he said, "Do you want these shelved in any particular order?"

"You don't have to do that," she protested. "I'll take care of them."

He put a hand on her shoulder, pressing lightly. "I'll do the heavy work," he said with a long, level look that temporarily kept her immobile. "You can do all the fine-tuning you want once they're on the shelves. Now, what's your system?"

Trying to work together in such close quarters wasn't the best idea in the world, she decided a few minutes later, staring blankly ahead. It took more concentration than she had to put her books in order while avoiding the touch of his rangy body.

After that quelling look, she had quietly moved out of his way, letting him do the donkey work. And now she sat cross-legged in front of the case while he hunkered down behind her, so close that she was warmed by his heat. Any other time she would have enjoyed the job before her. Normally nothing gave her more pleasure than handling books, savoring the touch and smell of them. But she never worked well with someone breathing down the back of her neck—especially someone sending out waves of sexual vibrations.

"Cody," she began in a faltering voice as his long arm came over her shoulder to touch one of the books. When his chest pressed against her back, she felt the heavy beat of his heart, then hers jolted and started to race in response. His hand dropped to trace the curve of her knee, then slowly moved up, trailing over the fabric on her thigh, and stopping briefly at her hip. It flattened over her belly, then rose to cup the fullness of her breast.

"What?" His mouth was near her ear, and he sounded as if he had been running. He wrapped his arm around her, his hand finding her other breast. Easing down behind her, he caught her earlobe between his teeth with soft aggression, and drew her back into the cradle of his thighs.

"Just...Cody," she managed, helplessly arching her back in instinctive invitation and pressing against his hands. Held within the grip of his muscular thighs, she felt the involuntary movement against her lower back, the hardening. Warmth spread through her, following the touch of his hands, coming from the heat of his big body. A strangled whimper left her throat, the raw, hungry sound shocking her to sudden stillness. It stopped her efforts to turn in his arms, to press against his hard chest, to taste his lips.

"Dear God, Cody, what are we doing?" she whispered in a ragged voice.

"Just what we've been heading for since the first day we met."

The flat, unequivocal statement restored her scattered senses in a hurry. "I haven't—"

"Maybe not intentionally," he cut in ruthlessly, lifting her easily and settling her across his hips so she was looking straight at him. "But our bodies don't always believe what we tell them, they react instinctively. And believe me, honey," he dipped his head and pressed a firm kiss on her parted lips, "your instincts are in great shape."

Liann blinked, breaking contact with those smoky, knowing eyes, wanting to deny his statement and knowing that she couldn't. She didn't *want* her instincts issuing orders, regardless of how subliminal they might be. She wanted her desires pushed down, covered up and buried, the way they'd been for the past two years. Life was more comfortable that way. Safer.

Some people might think that sounded dull and cowardly, she acknowledged, opening her eyes to find Cody's unwavering regard fixed on her. But to her, it sounded just fine. She didn't need a man stalking around the fringes of her life, ruffling her nerve endings and lighting her libido. What she *did* need was lots of space and flexibility, the freedom to do what she wanted when she wanted and to never again have to report her comings and goings to a possessive man. No, she assured herself, the more she thought about comfort and safety, the more appealing they sounded.

"You're a coward," Cody told her coolly.

"I haven't said a word!"

"You don't have to, your face tells me everything I need to know."

Liann tried to wiggle off his lap. She failed to do so because Cody locked his arm around her waist in gentle restraint. "All right," she said grudgingly, "I admit I'm...attracted to you. But it happens all the time. Two people meet, they're thrown in each other's company day after day and—"

"Are you saying that it's just a case of propinquity, that any man would do? That it's been two years since you left your husband and even I look good to you?" His hands slid to her waist and in one deft movement he set her on her feet. His voice was deliberately provoking.

"If you'd quit interrupting," she said wrathfully, watching him with a scowl as he got up, "you'd know you're not even close! What I'm trying to say is that whatever this thing is between us—"

"Attraction," he reminded her blandly.

"What*ever* it is," she said through gritted teeth, "it's not going to do either of us any good, so we might as well stop it right now."

He looked at her in fascination. "Just like that?"

"Look at it this way," she said reasonably. "You're only going to be here until October, November at the latest. Then you'll pack your things and take off for somewhere else. This is my home and I'll probably never leave it again except for brief trips. And if that isn't enough, you're a mainlander, and I'm a native."

"And never the twain shall meet?" His voice was wry as he absorbed the impact of her last statement.

"Something like that. I learned a hard lesson, Cody, and I learned it well. Some things just don't mix."

He moved back a step, leaning against the corner of his desk, giving her some breathing space. She shifted uneasily, almost wishing he hadn't. She knew where she stood when he came on like Attila the Hun, filled with straightforward aggression. That was bad enough, but it was when he got all cool and contained that he was the most dangerous, she realized with a start. Like now. He was like a hunter, patiently following his prey, allowing it time to think it had eluded its nemesis, to get careless—then springing the trap.

"And what about this thing between us that we'll call attraction for lack of a better word," he asked thoughtfully. "Aren't you even curious where it could lead?"

She dropped down in her chair, shaking her head. "I lost my curiosity about certain things the same time I lost my optimism about others."

"Coming from a lady who believes in myths and rainbows, that's a little hard to accept."

"Believe it," she said soberly. "You'll never hear a truer thing."

"I'll accept the fact that *you* believe it, but—"

A thump that sounded like a battering ram being thrust full force against the door jerked Cody's head around. "What the—"

"Yoo-hoo! Cody Hunter! Are you there?" The door shuddered beneath Lily's blows. "Aloha!"

Cupping Liann's chin in his hand, Cody leaned forward to drop a quick kiss on her upturned lips. "We're not through with this," he warned, wincing at the renewed pounding.

"Don't be so sure of that."

He took a long look at her stubborn expression before he reached for the doorknob. "I'm not letting you go through life thinking that the lessons you learned at that idiot's hands are the important ones," he promised grimly throwing open the door.

"Aloha, Cody Hunter." Lily swept in like a ship in full sail, the clashing colors of her muumuu almost blinding. Her hair was in a coronet of braids, the lines of her full face serene. "Aloha, Liann."

Liann answered absently, her gaze following Cody. The stiff set of his shoulders and the deliberate way he greeted his guest conveyed a warning that a cautious person shouldn't ignore, she decided. And since she definitely fell in that category, she wasn't about to provoke the aggressive male determination that rolled out of him in waves. Brooding about the nasty little surprises that life seemed to drop on unsuspecting souls, she moodily surveyed the man before her.

He was smiling at Lily, relaxed, humor narrowing his eyes and spreading a fan of tiny lines out from their corners. He really liked the old woman, she thought once again. In spite of all the hours of grief Lily had given him, he admired her for knowing what she wanted and her willingness to do battle for it. What it boiled down to, Liann decided, was that he recognized a kindred soul when he saw one. Because for sheer cross-grained perversity, hard-nosed stubbornness and pig-headed determination Lily had no equal, unless it was the man charming her right out of her scuffed flip-flops.

"Where I been?" Lily said, repeating Cody's question. "New birds coming, old birds going, something going on alla time, yeh? I been busy, you been busy, yeh? But I thought today I better see my friend Cody. See how he's gonna keep that big roof outta my way."

Sudden tension stiffened his shoulders. "Now, Lily, we've been through all that. You know I—"

A big hand fanned the air as she cut in. "I got my picture, Cody Hunter, and you got yours." Her gaze slid to Liann's face. "And Liann, she has hers. Maybe we all get what we want. Now," she said abruptly, getting down to business, "you got a mighty big hole dug out there." She nodded toward the sound of straining machinery. "I think maybe you gonna dig extra deep and put one more floor down there so the roof won't stick up so high. Yeh?" She spoke with unconscious authority, but there was a hopeful gleam in her eyes.

Cody shook his head, feeling the familiar knots of tension gather in his neck. "Lily," he said patiently, "when this building is finished, it's going to be beautiful. You'll be proud of it and it will serve a useful purpose. You already know all about the education center, the one Liann has been put in charge of. Its whole purpose is to contribute to the cultural revival, to help your people appreciate the pride and dignity of their heritage. But," he emphasized, "the building is going up exactly as it was designed. Not one thing is being changed."

Without a word, the slightly raffish woman sitting before him changed, the transformation making him believe every story he had heard about her royal ancestry. The expectancy in her gaze faded, leaving her intelligent eyes clear and as old as time itself. The lines on her face settled into a regal, aloof mask, the elegance of her posture a legacy of some distant training. Her aura of power was all the stronger for the fact that it was restrained. When she spoke, her words were precisely chosen, her voice refined. All in all, he realized with a sense of shock, she was one classy lady.

"I doubt that I will ever understand a system that builds a monument to culture with one hand and systematically destroys an ancient tradition with the other. However, Cody Hunter, I believe with all my heart and all my soul in the power of right. And it is right that my property and my tradition remain undisturbed. And somehow, perhaps in a way I have not yet considered, right will prevail. Be sure of that." She rose and glided to the door. "Aloha."

After the majestic exit, Liann wanted to stand up and cheer. "I feel like I just experienced the Fourth of July, Christmas and Easter all at the same time," she said in an awed voice.

Turning to her with a bemused expression, Cody said, "Yeah, I know what you mean. Aside from that, though, did you pick up anything else?"

Liann looked at him thoughtfully. "Such as?"

"A veiled threat?"

"Get serious, Cody. Why would Lily do something like that? She's crazy about you."

"She'd turn the hounds of hell loose on me if she thought it would help her," he said flatly. "And I couldn't blame her. I'd probably do the same thing myself if I were in her shoes."

"Flip-flops," Liann said absently, mulling over his words.

"Whatever."

She swiveled around in her chair, looking at the blank wall over her desk, trying to remember exactly what Lily had said. Something had jarred her as she listened, something that didn't quite ring true. Something that brought back images of the old Hawaiians, she thought, trying to recall the words the old woman had used. Cody's voice shattered the tenuous thread that was forming and she looked up irritably when he repeated his question.

"Did you?"

"Did I what?"

"Pick up on anything?"

"No. But I was listening to something else."

He moved over to stand by her desk, looking down in exasperation. "She wasn't here that long, and she didn't say that much. What else was there?"

"Something she didn't say," Liann said vaguely, turning back to the blank wall. No inspiration came and it wouldn't as long as Cody was staring down at her, probably wondering if she had lost her few remaining marbles. Ah, well, she decided philosophically, whatever it was, it would return in its own good time.

"Do you know what bird is a symbol of royalty, according to Hawaiian legend?" Liann asked Cody several evenings later. They were sitting in her living room after demolishing several cartons of Chinese food and half a bottle of wine.

The question roused him from his contemplation of her shapely legs. They both sat on the couch, separated by the width of a cushion, using the sturdy coffee table as a footrest. When he'd arrived with the bag of food, he caught her reading on her tiny *lanai*, wearing the same abbreviated pink shorts and top she'd been wearing the first time he had dropped in on her. This time, he thought with lazy contentment, she hadn't changed into something less revealing.

He could take at least partial credit for that, he decided with a touch of justifiable satisfaction. By mustering what little subtlety he was capable of, by letting his glance linger on her delightful bottom and thighs only when her back was turned, he reaped his reward.

"Well, do you?" she prodded.

"You're the expert on that stuff, why ask me?"

"It's the *'io*," she said triumphantly.

He stared at her, absorbing her expectant expression. "Is that supposed to mean something to me?"

"It's the Hawaiian hawk," she explained. "The bird that Auntie Lily has all over her house." She waited for him to make the connection.

"So? Undoubtedly she thinks it's beautiful. God knows, it is that," he said, remembering the grace and power of the photograph.

Liann shifted impatiently, turning toward him and folding one ankle beneath her thigh. Her hair fell softly around her shoulders and she threaded her fingers through it. "Or it could be that she really is of royal descent."

"Obviously I'm missing something here," he commented, aware of the excitement she was trying to suppress. It occurred to him again how easily read her emotions were, even—or especially—her reactions to him. He spared a quick moment of gratitude for that. It was one of the things that kept him sane through the long, dark nights when he ached to have her in bed beside him. She would probably allow her pretty, buffed nails to be torn out one by one before she'd admit it, but she wanted him. In spite of the fact that she wasn't always comfortable around him, that at times she was definitely wary of him and resented the sensual pull between them, she still wanted him.

"Don't you see, Cody? Most people are very proud to be descended from the *alii*, but she never mentions it. In fact, she puts on a very good act to cover it up. And, if that's the case, she may also very well be a *kahuna*!"

"Wait a minute." He unlaced his fingers from behind his head and sat up straighter. "It sounds to me like you're adding two and two and coming up with twenty-two. Besides, who really cares?"

"I do. And I'll admit that math was never one of my strong points, but I'm not that far off the mark."

"Liann," he began patiently.

Holding up a hand, palm toward him, she stopped him before he got off to a good start. "I know it's hard to understand, because I can't really explain it, but I have this feeling that—"

"Oh, God," he groaned, "you're not going to tell me another—"

"Cody." The word was said quietly, but it was a clear warning.

He dropped his head back to rest on the cushion and closed his eyes. "Okay, tell me about the feeling."

Now that she had his attention, as grudging as it was, Liann didn't quite know what to do with it. She had ideas, but no way to glue them together. She had suspicions but no real evidence. And she had a lot of suppositions with no logical conclusion. Not much to hand a man who seemed to thrive on structure and form.

"Tradition," she murmured. "She kept talking about tradition."

Cody rested his cheek on the cushion and opened one eye. "You sound like you're going to break into song at any minute."

"Don't get smart. Do you want some more wine?" she said absently, her thoughts obviously elsewhere. Without waiting for an answer, she got up and went to the kitchen.

Cody stared after her, not caring one way or another about the wine. He made a mental bet that she didn't either, that she was simply using it as an excuse to be by herself. It was a few minutes before she returned with a preoccupied expression and two glasses. She handed him one and curled up on the other end of the couch, staring down at the straw-colored liquid as if she could command pictures to appear on its surface.

Half an hour later, most of her wine was gone and she didn't look a bit happier. Cody was forcibly restraining himself, when she finally muttered, "This is ridiculous."

"What is?"

"I can't think. I've got all these fragments flying around in my head, but they won't settle down and make any sense."

"Maybe you're trying to work with too many of them at the same time. Isolate a couple of them and see what happens." He made himself comfortable, crossing his ankles on the table and resting the glass on his flat stomach. "Use me for a sounding board."

"You?" Her voice rose a notch.

"Me." He looked at her out of half-closed eyes, alerted by the surprised question. With her brown eyes wide open with doubt and her hair tumbling around her shoulders, she looked like a waif. A sexy waif. He wanted to pull her into his arms, stretch out on the couch with her next to him and wipe away all of her doubts. Even more than that, he discovered with a sense of shock, he wanted her to trust him enough to share her problems, her thoughts, even the ones that didn't make sense. Especially those, he realized, knowing suddenly that the man who had married and lost her had only possessed her body. With sudden, fierce determination, Cody knew that he wanted it all. He would settle for no less than everything.

"Try it," he murmured laconically. "It can't be any worse than what you're doing now."

She looked at him distractedly, obviously unnerved by his interest. He didn't move a muscle, waiting. The waif was going to have to sharpen her trusting mechanism and she might as well begin now.

"Where should I start?" she asked, crossing her legs yoga-style and folding her arms protectively in front of her.

"With a word, a phrase, an idea. I don't care."

"It's all so nebulous," she complained. "Your thinking is so nice and linear. You move so logically from *a* to *b* to *c*, and my mind just skitters all over the place, usually in circles."

"But you eventually get where you're going, don't you?" Cody's eyes were closed, his lips barely moving.

"Start with the hawk," he suggested when she made no response.

"Well, I already told you that it's a symbol of royalty."

"And that led you to Lily."

She nodded, then realized that he hadn't opened his eyes. "Um-hmm. I'm not sure why it's important, but I think it is."

"Bird," he said.

"Ah. They're all over the place. In artwork in Lily's home. Clustered by the thousands on her property. She talks to them, she prays for them, she's called the Bird Lady, and yet, I have the feeling that they're almost a cover-up for something else."

Gray eyes gleamed from beneath half-raised lashes. "What?"

She shrugged. "Beats me. Remember me telling you that words in our language have a number of meanings?" When he nodded, she said, "Our word for bird is *manu*. It also means any winged creature, or the tail of a kite."

"And where's that taking you?" he finally asked.

"Nowhere," she said with an impatient sigh. "Yet."

"Try another one. *Kahuna*."

"It means 'keeper of the secret,' and I guess I always think of Lily as having a lot of them."

"What kind of secrets?"

Slowly, by degrees, Liann relaxed. She scooted down toward Cody, propped a pillow against the arm of the couch and rested her head on it. "What kind do I think Lily has?"

He shook his head. "What kind did the *kahunas* have?"

"When they passed on their powers to another chosen person, they gave all the information they had. The secrets included all the sources of their power—traditions, sacred chants, everything."

"So we're back to traditions?"

Sighing, Liann said, "It's enough to drive you nuts, isn't it?"

"Maybe you're trying too hard."

"I never thought I'd hear you say something like that."

"Why not?" Cody sat up, placed his glass carefully on the table, and turned, wrapping his arms around her bent knees. Looking down at her startled face, he said, "I'm a great believer in letting my subconscious do its share. I do all the legwork, collect all the data, then I just let it perk for a while. Believe it or not, I get most of my brilliant ideas first thing in the morning, before I'm fully awake."

Liann took a sudden sharp breath, aware of the predatory gleam in Cody's smoky eyes. The light from the lamp silvered his thick hair, leaving her with an overwhelming desire to touch it. She slipped her fingers into it, slowly shaping his head with her hands.

Liann, she told herself as she lightly massaged his temples with her thumbs, you're playing with fire. You're going to regret this in the morning.

With uncharacteristic impulsiveness she sat up and slid her arms around his neck. What the hell, she thought, every woman should play with fire at least once in her life!

Chapter Eight

When Liann's lips brushed lightly against his, Cody wasted about one second debating whether or not to act the gentleman, then his body reacted instinctively before his brain presented its vote. Wrapping his arms around her slim waist, he allowed her slight weight to press him backward until he lay full length on the couch, holding her firmly in place on top of him. One hand slid down to anchor her hips, the other locked in place at her nape.

Her cool lips tasted of wine, the light, slightly sweet flavor of a French champagne he'd once tried. An intoxicating concept, he thought whimsically, the tip of his tongue touching the corner of her mouth. His Irish-Hawaiian lady full of French champagne and spread over an English Boston Brahmin like frosting on a cake. He almost groaned aloud with the sheer pleasure of it. Her breasts pressed softly against him; her hips and thighs were a resilient shelter for his growing hardness.

Even as he teased her full lower lip gently with his teeth, he knew it wouldn't be long before his state of arousal transmitted itself to her, and then an even shorter span of time before she tried to reverse her impulsive decision.

Remembering the combination of anxiety and recklessness on her face as she twined her fingers in his hair, he knew her rush of shy daring would soon be over. Not about to let her retreat, he deepened the kiss. At the same time, he reached out and nudged the coffee table away from the couch. Locking his ankles around hers, he slid from the sofa, took the weight of the fall on his shoulder and hip then rolled to a stop.

Liann's lashes lifted, revealing surprised brown eyes that stared up at him. "Cody?"

"Shhh," he whispered, resting his weight on his forearms, his hips pressing her to the carpet. "Now it's my turn." Lacing his fingers in the silky mass of hair at her temples, he smoothed her brows with his thumbs, a fierce hunger surging through him for this sweet, sweet woman. Her tumbled hair formed a luxuriant fan against the deep pile of the carpet and he had an instant image of how it would look on the pillows of his bed. Glorious. Sexy. Bewitching.

Each time he held her in his arms he knew that one day he would have her. This time was no exception. She was going to belong to him, he vowed, just as surely and completely as he would belong to her. He took a ragged breath and lowered his head.

Just before his lips touched hers, a small shiver of panic shook Liann. Part of the reason for her uncharacteristically aggressive gesture, or so she told herself, had been to show him that she was in control, that she could end the embrace whenever she felt it was prudent to do so. Unfortunately, she had lost sight of that goal before it had become fully developed. So much for assertive behavior, she thought wryly, hazily aware that she was sandwiched between the plush rug and Cody's hard body.

Whatever protest she'd intended to make was muffled by his lips. But, as always, there was nothing rough or demanding about Cody's kisses. And, as always, they held multiple levels of emotions. They whispered of passion, of giving and taking. They spoke of a bonding never to be broken. They called to her, quietly encouraging her to trust. They reminded her that life demanded the glory of rainbows. And they dazzled her with the force of desire. His desire? Hers? It was all the same, she realized. It was impossible to know where one left off and the other began. It was exactly the same with their bodies. They fit with precision, her curves flowing into his hardness, only the clothes they wore keeping them apart.

Startled at the realization, she put her hands on his shoulders and applied pressure. Eventually her message got through to Cody. Slowly, reluctantly, he raised his head and blinked. A satisfied gleam appeared in his eyes when he examined her flushed face.

She took a deep breath, trying to ignore the fact that her breasts nudged his chest, and exhaled. "Cody." She stopped and cleared her throat. "We've got to talk."

"Now?" He settled his weight more heavily on his forearms and waited warily for her response.

"Yes." She wiggled, testing the extent of her captivity. "You wouldn't consider moving, would you?" she asked politely.

His sudden grin was rueful. "Not just at the moment. It would help if you didn't squirm around like that. What do you want to talk about?"

Her sigh was full of exasperation. "What do you think? You. Me." She waved a hand that encompassed their melded bodies. "Us!"

"Okay, shoot."

"I'd like to," she muttered. "Cody, get up! You're squashing me."

He bent down and kissed the tip of her nose. "Woman, you have no soul."

"That's squashed too," she said firmly. "Move! And don't call me woman."

Shifting carefully, making sure that he didn't hurt her, Cody rolled to his side. Propping his cheek on a fist, he said, "Why interrupt what we were doing for a discussion? We were already involved in some, uh, high-level communication."

"You've got things turned around," she said, sitting up and crossing her legs. "It was the interrupting part I wanted to talk about. I thought we agreed that this was going to have to stop."

Cody stared at her, an expression of polite interest on his face.

"Didn't we?"

"Nope."

"What do you mean 'nope'? We *did* talk about it."

Cody rolled to his back, lacing his fingers behind his head, and contemplated the ceiling. "You talked, I listened."

"I distinctly remember that we discussed our differences—"

He shook his head. "You did."

"—and we agreed that—"

"Not true."

"—things wouldn't work—"

He shook his head again.

"—between us."

"Wrong."

"*Wrong?*"

"And you know it." He stared at her outraged expression, not giving an inch. "There isn't one of those problems that can't be resolved with a little discussion and compromise." Sitting up in one lithe movement, he added softly, "They're excuses, Liann. You took a gamble once and lost, so now you're afraid to try again."

"That's not true!"

"Isn't it?" he asked, getting to his feet. "I think it is. Think about it."

Having Cody drop conversational bombs before walking out the door was getting to be a habit, Liann reflected as she pulled into the parking area of the work site several mornings later. A nasty one that she hoped he didn't plan to cultivate. He was hard enough to cope with under normal circumstances; she hated to think what he'd be like if he polished up that particular technique.

She had almost reached the trailer when the quiet penetrated her consciousness. For a workday, the noise level was unusually low, almost nonexistent, in fact. Walking through the gate in the chain link fence, she found Cody in conversation with Hal, the foreman.

"I don't know, Cody," the tall, thin man was saying, staring at a sheaf of messages clutched in his callused hand. "They all called in." He read the names written on the pink slips.

"Are they sick?"

"Not exactly." After one glance at Cody's stony face, his slow speech revved up a few notches. "What I mean is, *they* aren't sick, but someone is."

Cody's eyes narrowed, and a look of disbelief spread across his face. "Wait a minute. You're telling me that other people are sick and eight of my men are staying home? Why, for God's sake?"

"The word I got was that the *tutus*, the old folks," he explained for Cody's benefit, "are sick and needed to be taken to the doctor. Same thing in each case. And there wasn't anyone else at home to do it."

Cody swore. "See if you can get some men to come in and work for the day." When he turned away, Liann paced along beside him. His gaze prowled around the area, touching here and there, making sure that everything else was running smoothly.

"I know this blows a big hole in your schedule," she murmured in a comforting tone, "but it isn't all that unusual. We take care of our old people here."

"Has a flu epidemic hit the island?" he asked suddenly.

She tucked her arm through his, shaking her head. "Not that I know of. Why?"

"Because the same thing happened yesterday, and the day before."

Liann dropped her hand from his arm and stared up at him, a startled frown drawing her brows together. *What on earth was going on?* She knew the men who hadn't shown up for work; in fact she was related to a good number of them. Which meant that in one way or another she was related to their elderly aunts, uncles and grandparents. She hadn't heard of any illness running rampant through the family.

Just the evening before she had visited her parents
and they hadn't said a word—and they would have
known. On the island, large families had a networking
system that put the CIA to shame, everyone knew
everything about everyone else. In the Murphy family,
Sean and Mei's house was the center of the web. They
coordinated the informal but large information re-
trieval system and knew, long before many of the events
were made public, who was engaged, who *should* have
been engaged, who was married, pregnant, ill or in the
throes of a divorce. She made a mental note to check
with her parents. Soon.

Slowly, she followed Cody to the trailer where he had
been summoned to the telephone. She walked through
the door just in time to hear his end of a very peculiar
conversation.

"Yes, Mr. Lee, how are you? Good. Fine. Thank
you, it's a pleasure doing business with you, too."

Smiling at Cody's efforts to match Mr. Lee's exqui-
site courtesies, she dropped down into her chair and
crossed her legs. Mr. Lee was an old friend of the family, old being the operative word. He was ancient. He
was also an astute businessman who was in his office
each morning when his employees arrived, and stayed
long after they had left. His industry had paid off years
earlier, resulting in a business of enormous scope. Devin
and Megan, the youngest Murphys, had somewhat ir-
reverently named him the mortar magnate. Mr. Lee was
the man that the island people called when they needed
cement. Jobs ranging in size from a hotel on Waikiki
Beach to a private swimming pool on Kauai were all
personally handled by Mr. Lee.

"I beg your pardon."

Blinking at the icy challenge in Cody's voice, Liann leaned forward in concern, waving her hands frantically. It wasn't any wiser to mess with Mr. Lee than it was to annoy Madame Pele. Not if you wanted your cement delivered.

"Why?"

The flat, single word wasn't much of an improvement, she reflected glumly, at least not in her opinion. It sounded extremely hostile.

"The forms will be finished tomorrow. How long?" If anything, Cody's expression grew grimmer. His fierce stare told Liann that he wasn't about to hand over the phone so that she could make polite noises into it. "I'm sorry, too," he said finally. "I expected more from you and your company."

"Cody," Liann said, scandalized, as he replaced the receiver with angry precision. "How could you talk to Mr. Lee that way?"

"It was easy."

"What on earth has he done?"

"Rescheduled the delivery of the cement." The control in his voice as he pulled a thick file of papers out of a drawer told her exactly how furious he was.

"Why?"

He shrugged. "A shortage of supplies, a truck strike, he's got no end of reasons."

"Believe me," she said earnestly, "he wouldn't have done it if he'd had any alternative. Mr. Lee is a man of his word. His reputation is solid gold."

"That may be," he said tersely, "but his job is to deliver my cement. Mine is to see that I get the Center finished on or before schedule."

"How late is it going to be?"

"Two days."

"If there's a way to get it for you, he'll do it."

Her words didn't noticeably soothe him, she reflected, watching him reach for the telephone. Several
minutes and several calls later, they had both learned
something. Cody discovered what she already knew: if
Mr. Lee didn't have cement, nobody did. Liann's insight went a bit deeper.

In a crisis, Cody was not a man who wasted time or
energy on displays of temper. When he was confronted
with a problem, he simply looked for a solution. When
he found one, his mind went into overdrive, investigat-
ing and weighing the pros and cons. He was resource-
ful and had the determination of a bloodhound. She
wasn't surprised. Judging from the way he handled situations in his personal life, she had suspected that was
exactly how he would react. It was nice to have her
conclusions validated, she thought, watching him re-
place the receiver once again.

On the other hand, she reflected uneasily as his un-
blinking gaze settled on her crossed legs, it reinforced
another thought that had been revolving around her
brain with unnerving frequency. Cody wasn't a man
who took no for an answer easily, if at all. He reminded her of one of those weighted, inflatable men
that kids used for a punching bag. When you delivered
your best shot and thought the bag was down for the
count, it rolled right back to its feet and was ready to go
another round.

"Any luck?" she asked as he dropped the receiver
back in the cradle yet again.

"No."

"What are you going to do?"

He shrugged and attached a sheaf of papers to a
large, battered clipboard. "Figure some way to work

around it. I'll see you later, I've got to go out and talk to Hal.''

"Wait a minute. I probably won't be here when you get back," she reminded him. "This is the day I'm going to Pahala to interview that old lady who used to work in the sugar mill."

"When do you think you'll be back?"

"It'll be late. I'll probably go straight home. Are you coming to my folks' place for dinner?"

He nodded. "What time?"

"The usual. Whenever you get there. Any time after six," she amended hastily, remembering his off-island standards of propriety. The last thing she wanted to do right now was to get involved in a long discussion about guests who show up too early or too late for social functions.

Late that afternoon, she headed home from Pahala, thinking about the interview with Mrs. Hasegawa, recalling the woman's button-bright eyes and hands gnarled from years of hard work. Although she appeared to be Japanese, she was actually Japanese-Hawaiian. On her Hawaiian side, Mrs. Hasegawa's grandmother had helped rear her, sharing with her a wealth of wisdom and folklore.

The process of interviewing or "talking story" was one that always fascinated Liann and she had persisted until the Institute allowed her to establish a department specializing in oral history interviews with senior citizens. Unexpected benefits had resulted from the project. It had, of course, enriched Liann's research, but it went far beyond that. Senior citizens who had once been the subjects of interviews volunteered to seek out and interview others, and now there was a large core group involved.

Once the old people overcame their shyness, they
spoke uninhibitedly about folklore and their early lives.
They talked about evil spirits and ghosts, legends,
stories and experiences.

And once in a great while, something wonderful
happened.

Liann reached down to touch a bulky package resting on the seat beside her. At the end of the interview,
Mrs. Hasegawa had said hesitantly, "My daughter said
I should tell you that I have several old notebooks written by my grandmother, Maile Kalama. She was educated at a missionary school and wrote of many things.
If you are interested in them, I will be happy to show
you."

Interested? Liann caught a glimpse of her deliriously
happy smile in the rearview mirror and hoped that she
had given a fairly professional answer to the old
woman. It was a researcher's dream to find written
documents. The excitement rose in quantum leaps if the
person writing them was well educated and a keen ob-
server of the times. Mrs. Hasegawa's grandmother not
only met, she surpassed both qualities. Aside from that,
she was a great storyteller.

Liann laughed aloud, remembering how avidly she
had skimmed the pages and finally turned to her bewil-
dered hostess and *begged* permission to borrow the four
volumes. Now that she had them, she was itching to dig
into them. Casting a quick glance at her watch, she estimated that she should get home in time to shower,
wash her hair and dress and still have a couple of hours
to read before meeting Cody at her parents' house.

Cody's eyes were all over her. He met her halfway
between the pool and the house and took her hand.

"Whatever it is," he said, indicating her dress, "it's a knockout."

Liann looked down at the muted pink *pareu*. Smiling at him she said, "What, this?"

As if he were leading her in a dance, he drew her in a small circle before him. "Yeah, that," he said finally in a voice that ruffled her nerve endings. "No zipper, no buttons that I can see. What keeps it up?"

"Technique. Actually," she hurriedly explained, made unaccountably nervous by his steady stare, "it's just a long strip of material. How you fold it determines the style."

He eyed the strapless affair with new interest. The material cupped her breasts in a way that made his palms tingle. The way it stretched across her fetching little bottom put thoughts in his head that could lead him to a lot of grief. The rest of it gathered in a graceful fold that stretched from her breasts to her knees. "I like your style," he said finally.

"Thanks. Now," she said lightly, determined to change the subject to something less personal, "I know for a fact that we won't be eating for at least an hour. Who would you like to meet?"

"No one."

"Cody, these get-togethers serve a number of purposes. Aside from the food, they offer old friends a chance to visit, business people an opportunity to network a little and adversaries some neutral ground." She grabbed his arm and steered him back to the house. "I think you should talk to Mr. Lee."

He dug in his heels and brought her to a stop. "I already did that."

Her eyes widened in surprise. "You did?"

"Um-hmm."

When he just stood there like a clam, she tugged on his shirt and said impatiently, "Well, what happened?"

"He apologized for disappointing me."

She winced. "Ouch."

"And I apologized for being rude enough to admit my disappointment."

Her brows shot up. "Classy. I'm impressed."

"So was he, apparently. He told me I'd have my concrete tomorrow, after all."

Liann said thoughtfully, "Something serious must have happened to make him call you this morning. Mr. Lee isn't a capricious person, especially when it concerns business."

"I agree. He probably pulled out some big guns to settle the matter."

As they talked, Liann tucked her arm through his and got him moving again. Before they reached the house, Megan, her red hair turned into a radiant halo by the long, early evening rays of sunlight, descended on them.

"There you are," she said cheerfully, capturing Cody's other arm. Peering across the width of his chest, she said to her sister, "About twenty female relatives are demanding to meet Cody. I think they want to check him out before they start beating the bushes for eligible males for you." Glancing up, she gave Cody a limpid smile, saying, "They believe it's time that she get her feet wet again."

Cody's gaze took in the resigned expression on Liann's face before switching to Megan. Mischief gleamed in her eyes, and a challenge. He released Liann's arm, wrapped his hand around her nape and dropped a swift, thoroughly possessive kiss at the corner of her mouth.

"I have a few thoughts on the subject myself," he said thoughtfully, turning to the vivid youngster.

"Cody," Liann said warningly, "don't you dare embarrass me."

"Me?" He was the picture of injured innocence. "I wouldn't dream of it. I'm just going to let them know you've already dipped your toe in the water."

"That's it?" She narrowed her eyes in suspicion.

He nodded. "And that you fell in up to your armpits."

"*Cody.*"

"See you at dinner." He nudged Megan toward the house. "After all," his voice drifted back to Liann, "we wouldn't want them to expend a lot of unnecessary energy, would we?"

Liann watched them walk away, torn by the knowledge that he *was* going to embarrass her and the realization that she didn't care nearly as much as she would have the week before. Also, there was a measure of relief. She had been heading back to the house so she could foist Cody off on someone, anyone, for a half hour or so. She needed to talk to Uncle Loe.

She searched the house room by room until she spied his familiar thatch of steel-gray hair. He was having a conversation with one of her aunts. Moving through the crowded room, she came to a halt beside the slim man, waiting for a lull in the discussion. When it came, she smiled at her aunt and said, "I need to kidnap Uncle Loe for a while if you don't mind."

Liann took his hand and led him outside toward the pool. Pointing to a couple of secluded chairs, she said, "Are these okay?" Uncle Loe nodded for her to be seated before he eased himself down. He waited patiently, allowing her to collect her thoughts.

"Today I had an interview with a Mrs. Hasegawa in Pahala," she said abruptly.

"An enjoyable one, I hope."

She nodded, brushing away the polite inquiry. Her uncle was extremely courteous; they would spend the entire evening exchanging pleasantries if she wasn't careful. "Very nice," she said, "but that isn't what I want to talk about."

"Then tell me."

She breathed a sigh of relief. He was also as sharp as he was good-natured. He knew she wouldn't have dragged him away from the others unless it was important. And in his own blessed way, he never made judgments on what "important" might be. It was enough that it mattered to her.

"Mrs. Hasegawa loaned me several books," she explained, glancing at her watch and speaking swiftly. Privacy was vastly underrated around the Murphys and someone was bound to interrupt them before long. "They were written long ago by her grandmother, who was educated by the missionaries. The books are wonderful and I'm going to cherish every moment spent studying them, but tonight before I came here I read something that bothered me. I need your help, Uncle Loe."

A guarded look came into his eyes. "There are some things that are not mine to tell. You of all people know that."

Liann nodded. She did know. To be a "keeper of the secret" was an awesome responsibility. One did not violate the strictures imposed.

"Then let me tell you what I know," she said softly, "and we'll talk about it. Isn't it true that the old ways taught that there was one essential condition to observe when praying?"

"And that is?" he prompted.

"That the prayer not hurt someone else. The only real sin was in hurting another's feelings or coveting his possessions."

He nodded. "You remember your lessons well."

"Uncle Loe, thoughts are coming to me with the speed of hummingbirds in flight. Bits and pieces that I can't connect. And if I don't, I'm afraid that a good person is going to be very badly hurt."

"Tell me."

"In my search for legends, I came across fragments of information. Some make connections, some don't. The ones that don't float around in my head waiting to find a home."

He nodded again, a sign that said "I may not *tell*, but I can listen."

"You know how I've always felt about the legend I call the Valley of Rainbows, that the true ending has not yet been discovered?"

"You've told me your theories many times." His smile reminded her of the hours he had spent listening while she theorized and tried to deduce something from his expressions.

"Today, I found something in that book that convinced me. I know I'm right."

His brows raised in inquiry.

"Mrs. Hasegawa's grandmother wrote the legend in her book. It was almost word for word as I know it, ending with the line about finding their valley, the heart of their dreams. But there was one difference."

"What was that?"

"There was a note that said the rest of the story belongs to the Keeper of the Golden Bird."

Bingo, Liann thought triumphantly, watching a flicker of surprise appear in her uncle's eyes. It was gone as quickly as it came, but she had seen it.

"What do you know of this Keeper of—what did you call it—the Golden Bird?" Uncle Loe's expression changed from inscrutable to avuncular interest.

Well done, she applauded silently. Just the right amount of hesitancy in the question, the perfect degree of intellectual interest on his face. "That's the name," she agreed blandly. "And I know very little."

"But you think there is such a person?"

"I'm sure of it."

"Even now?"

"Even now."

"After all these years?"

"After all these years."

"Why?"

"Because of other bits and pieces."

"And what do you want from me?"

"A name."

He shook his head, a faint smile moving his lips. "I have not said I believe in such a person."

"Uncle Loe," she said urgently, "my bits and pieces aren't coming together quickly enough to prevent a great hurt. If I knew, I might be able to do something about it."

"Some things are meant to be," he said philosophically, slowly getting to his feet. "Others are not."

"Uncle Loe," she wailed, "I can't just sit and do nothing."

"There are some who can't," he agreed. "And you are one of them."

"What can I do?"

"Use what you have been given."

"The book?"

"That too."

"What else?" she asked quickly, seeing Cody walking toward them.

"Your brain, your instincts, your powers of reasoning. Potent weapons in one who also cares."

Chapter Nine

The next morning Liann stepped out on her *lanai* clad in the thigh-length white silk shirt she wore as a robe. She carried one of Maile Kalama's notebooks in one hand and a dish of cut fruit in the other. When she moved through the sliding glass doors, her gaze went, as it invariably did, to the impossibly green grass sloping down to the slabs of lava rock. There was no beach there, no rolling surf, just deep water surging against the wall of black rock. Home, she thought, with the usual twist of inner contentment. Whatever part of the island she was on, she was home.

But this morning, instead of lingering over the fragrant scents, the familiar sounds, the merging blues of the water and the sky, she pulled out a chair and sat down at the glass-topped table. Before opening the book, she glanced at her watch and practically purred. Most mornings at this time, she would be eating a hurried breakfast and preparing to leave for work. But today, thanks to Cody, she didn't have to be anywhere.

A grin curved her lips when she remembered telling him last night at dinner about the miraculous appearance of Maile Kalama's journals. No, "telling" was understating the case, she reflected wryly. She had gone on for twenty minutes or so, at top speed, hardly letting the poor man eat. Finally, probably in self-defense, he had suggested that she spend the following day working at home.

A day of uninterrupted reading, she thought, blinking in awe. She could hardly believe it. But it wouldn't do to get carried away with gratitude, she warned herself. Cody's generosity wasn't completely devoid of selfish motives. She had a sneaking suspicion that he'd known she was planning to leave her parents' house early and return to her place so she could dip into those precious volumes, and that was the one thing he didn't want her to do.

Cody, it seemed, had a vested interest in keeping her at the gathering. According to Megan, he had made the rounds of her matchmaking relatives and subtly staked his claim. Once that was done, obviously he had to keep her around and make the story look good!

"He's a crafty man," Megan had told her with a low laugh, refusing to say what his exact words had been to the women. "But believe me," she added, round eyed with remembrance, "he stopped them dead in their tracks." Her laughter had turned into an irrepressible giggle at Liann's groan.

Determinedly Liann put aside thoughts of last night. She had been given an entire day, and she'd be a fool not to take advantage of the time granted her. As a precaution, she ate the chunks of papaya and pineapple quickly and moved the dish out of the way before reaching for the book.

Maile Kalama was a credit to her missionary teachers, Liann reflected. Her handwriting was painstakingly neat, her powers of observation acute and her ability to express herself was extraordinary. The books were written as journals more than anything else; they were charming collections of daily events interspersed with legends and bits of wisdom.

It was midmorning when Liann finished the first one. She turned the last page with a half-smile of regret. Maile was her kind of woman: curious, always asking questions and then taking the answers with a grain of salt. She was also uncommonly interested in legends. She seemed to write some down just for the pleasure of transcribing the flowing poetic phrases, others because she was afraid they might be forgotten by the next generation.

Liann took the chronicle inside and placed it on the table next to the others. She was standing there, taking pleasure from the fact that she still had three unread volumes before her when the telephone rang. She reached out to answer it without removing her eyes from the thick notebooks.

"Hello."

"Are you having fun?" Cody asked. The rough texture of his voice came through the line with an intimacy that momentarily stunned her.

"I'm having a wonderful time," she said cheerfully, pulling herself together. She wondered absently if Cody Hunter's voice would always send the blood roaring through her head, creating such a din.

"Good. I'm glad someone is."

"What do you mean?" she asked, not sure she wanted to know.

"Nothing. Or at least nothing I can't handle."

Now Liann knew for sure she didn't want to hear. "Do you need me?" she asked, resigned to hear the worst.

"I always need you."

Liann shivered, aware that her body was reacting to the flat statement. It was hard to remain objective about his words, she reflected, when her hands tingled and her pulse rate leaped into overdrive. "Cody," she said warningly, "I'm talking business here. What's happening down there?"

"Nothing. Now."

"I can't stand enigmatic men," she told him. "Talk."

Instead, he asked, "Remember when your uncle did the blessing here?"

"Of course." A flicker of unease ran down her spine.

"You said he pulled out all the stops. Did the coverage include willful mischief as well as spirit-world shenanigans?"

"That does it. I'm getting dressed and coming down there."

"Dressed?"

She grinned at the sudden interest in his voice.

"It's almost noon. What have you got on?"

"Don't exaggerate," she told him briskly. "It's only ten-thirty. And I'm wearing my robe."

"Oh." In the pause that followed, she could almost see him considering the sunshine and realizing that it was too warm for a robe. "Tell me what it looks like," he ordered suddenly.

"What is this?" she demanded, her grin widening at the anticipation in his voice. "One of those heavy-breathing calls?"

"That good, huh? Maybe I'll come over."

"And maybe you won't. You were telling me about your problems," she reminded him. There was a distinct pause that warned her she was about to receive a heavily edited version of the morning's events.

"More men are out," he said finally. "For the same reason. And the keys for all the trucks and heavy equipment were gone from my desk this morning."

"I don't understand," she finally managed. "Sammy's there at night. How could they disappear?"

"Good question. The very one that I asked him."

"And?" she prodded impatiently. "What'd he say?"

"He told me straight for two solid hours that no one took them." Exasperation roughened his voice when he added, "At least no one from this world. He's not so sure about the other one. He said everything was quieter than usual last night. Some time around midnight a couple of his friends dropped by. He let them in and they talked for a while, but he vouches for them."

"Who were they?" she asked curiously. Sammy would be very selective about who he let inside the gates.

"Willard Chan and Joe Freitas."

"They're nice old guys," she assured him. "Insomniacs. They often go for late walks together. So what did you do about the keys?"

"Got duplicates for the heavy equipment locking devices from a local dealer. Had a locksmith come out for the trucks. It only took a couple of hours."

A couple of hours that he resented spending, she knew. Time that should not have been wasted. "So is there anything I can do?" she asked, rephrasing her earlier question.

"No. I just wanted to hear your voice."

"Oh." She was disconcerted. What was worse, she was certain that he knew she was. And he wasn't doing anything to break the awkward silence. "Well," she said uncertainly, "I guess we might as well go back to work."

"I guess so." He sounded like a cat with cream on its face, she thought in disgust. "Dinner tonight?" he asked abruptly.

"Fine. Not too early, though."

"I'll be by around seven."

She replaced the receiver slowly, realizing that she hadn't even hesitated before accepting the invitation. Slowly but surely Cody was filling all the empty hours of her life. Shrugging, she thought about what he'd said. More bits and pieces, she reflected. And none of them made sense. She had talked with the men who had called in sick before. Paranoid as it sounded, she had wondered if there was some sort of conspiracy in the making. Each man had assured her that his absence was legitimate, and she believed him. An elderly family member had been ill and had needed care. And according to the latest report from Cody, the mysterious malady was still making the rounds.

Then there was Mr. Lee. It was interesting that even though he had apologized, he had never explained. Add Mr. Chan and Mr. Freitas to the list, and what do you have? she asked herself. A lot of nice old people. Of course, that didn't mean a thing. The island was full of nice old people. If she were to think that there was some grand scheme afoot, she was indeed toying with paranoia.

Enough of that. Not only was it ridiculous, but it was also undermining her faith in human nature. If you can't trust the *tutus*, who can you trust? Unwilling to deal with the unanswerable, she picked up another journal and settled down in the corner of the couch.

Late that afternoon, Liann carefully turned the next fragile page—and simply stopped breathing. She re-read the few, brief lines. Blinking, she read them again. They stood by themselves, apropos of nothing at all.

"I don't believe it," she whispered. When she least expected it, was she actually being given the gift of a lifetime?

From its soaring ascent in a dark and quiet world to its descent in silent majesty, the flight of the golden bird is constant. Sharing its mana with all, kingly in power and grace, the golden bird has no rival. Bestowing constant benediction, the keeper of the golden bird is graced beyond measure.

Liann closed the large book and placed it carefully on the cushion beside her. Folding her legs tailor fashion and resting her head on the back of the sofa, she closed her eyes and took a deep breath. She forced herself to remain like that until she calmed her rapid breathing and stilled the tumultuous thoughts ricocheting in her head. Now, she told herself, think.

Slowly, as if she was piecing together a gigantic jigsaw puzzle, she sifted through the maze of ideas and fragments of thought, removing them one at a time and interlocking each with the other until gradually, a picture formed. When it was complete, she opened her eyes and stared at her bookshelves, at the books from which she had learned so much. Doubt shook her for a moment. Then she slowly shook her head. No, her picture was right. She knew it. Now all she had to do was prove it.

Liann turned off the rutted road and stopped beside a mud-splashed Blazer. Before she had time to close the car door behind her, Lily was on the porch smiling a greeting.

"Aloha, Liann. You been making good pictures?"

"Aloha, Auntie." Liann reached the stairs and smiled gravely at the old woman. "Yes, I've been making pictures."

"Ha, I see you watch Cody Hunter with big eyes. You never tell me that your pictures be about a big white building."

"No, Auntie," she admitted, "mine have been about other things."

"Ah, well," Lily said comfortably, shooing Liann in ahead of her, "Cody Hunter is a fair man. This old woman will have her picture, just you wait and see." She dropped down in a massive chair and stared at Liann. "You're not going to be a fool and let him go, are you?"

Noting absently that Auntie had slid into another role, leaving her fractured English behind, Liann asked curiously, "Would I be such a fool?"

"Yes. He looks at you with his heart in his eyes."

"And how do I look at him?"

"The same way. You can trust this one," the old woman said flatly.

"I know." And she did know, she realized suddenly. Her heart, her life, her future were all safe in his hands. Tucking the thought away for later, she said softly, "You're behind the goings-on down at the site, aren't you?"

The old woman looked out through the open door. When she spoke, it was without apology. "They were only minor inconveniences, nothing that would harm him. Merely delaying tactics."

"Why?"

"I wanted him to have more time to think. Of course, that was only part of it," she admitted, smiling rue-fully at her own failings. "There is also the fact that I can't resist meddling. I know the power of my pictures, I know I need do nothing else. I tell others how to do it, tell them to trust, but do I take my own advice?"

Liann shook her head, grinning at the other wom-an's wry admission. "Obviously not."

"Of course not. I often had my father in despair. Patience, he would tell me. Wait, and all will come to you as long as you practice what I teach." Grinning suddenly, she said, "You would think that an old lady would know better, yeh?"

"Speaking of old ladies," Liann said carefully, "and old gentlemen, would you tell me how you got half the island involved in your little plan? I assume the sudden breakout of unexplained illnesses was all a part of it?"

Auntie nodded cheerfully.

"And Mr. Lee?"

"That was a hard one. I asked much of him."

"And Mr. Chan and Mr. Frietas?"

"Good friends, both of them. All of them. All of them willing to help."

"Why did they do it, Auntie?" Liann asked. "Was it more than friendship?"

The older woman stared out the door again, seeing something invisible to younger eyes. "Because," she finally said, "we share...a history, you might say. We remember the same things. Things that are more important than telling a harmless story to strong young men who will leave their work for a day because they have kind hearts. More important than the embarrassment a businessman suffers when telling a customer that his supplies will be late. More important than two sleepless men tricking a friend and taking something that will be returned the next day."

"What things, Auntie?"

"Teachings that were not passed on to the young, customs that have dimmed with time, beliefs that have faded from many memories. Times that changed our world and left us relics of the past."

Nodding in understanding, Liann reached out and touched the wood carving on the table beside her. "Tell me about this," she requested softly, knowing they still had a lot of ground to cover, and that it was going to be an uphill battle all the way.

The other woman blinked, apparently surprised at the turn in the conversation. "About the *'io*?" she asked, her eyes following Liann's finger as it gently traced the curved beak.

"Um-hmm."

"What's to tell?" Auntie asked with a massive shrug. "It's a beautiful bird, especially in flight. As you can see," she said with a broad gesture that took in the entire room, "it is my favorite of all the birds."

"It's found only on this island, isn't it?"

"Only on this one," Auntie agreed.

"Legend has it that the *'io* is a symbol of royalty," Liann said, wondering if her bait would be taken.

"I have heard that, too," Auntie said calmly. "If true, it would be most fitting. Hawks in flight have a regal quality known to few other birds."

"Their coloring is quite beautiful. Would you call them golden birds?"

The massive form across from her stilled. Brown eyes swept over her, examining her look of polite inquiry. "No," the old woman said finally, "they might look that way from a distance, but they are actually brown with almost white chests. Only their feet and legs are yellow."

"You have them throughout your house," Liann commented carefully. "One would wonder if there was some significance in the fact."

Auntie's laugh was a comfortable sound. "Yes, indeed. It means that I am blessed with many friends who know of my preference. Each, according to his or her talent, presents me with a gift that I will cherish. Am I not fortunate?"

"Indeed," Liann said dryly, replacing the carving on the table. Not only fortunate, but wily as an old fox.

Liann got up and walked over to the door, watching the lengthening shadows work their way across the yard. It wasn't long until sunset, she estimated. Only about another half hour. If she was right, Lily would either have to get rid of her or break a lifetime of silence. For a fleeting moment, she almost wished the regal old lady would come up with one of her inventive ploys, delaying the inevitable moment. Then common sense intervened. If Lily was to have the one thing vital to her life, it had to come.

Looking over her shoulder, she said, "Auntie, you've never told me about your childhood. What was it like?"

"A golden time," the old woman said with a sigh, her face serene with distant memories. "Busy, structured, time for learning, time for laughter."

Liann's head bowed as she absently contemplated the thonged sandals that had so fascinated Cody. For more years than she cared to count, she had studied island legends, reading them with an empathy that was part and parcel of her life. Biologically and emotionally, she was tied to these people born of the sea, these people who lived on islands shaped by fire.

She had been reared to believe in destiny. Part of hers, she had known, was to find and share with her people the ending of the legend of rainbows. And now it was within her grasp, for with those few words about her childhood, Lily had just paid her the ultimate compliment: that of knowledge and understanding. Most people would have taken the statement at face value, she reflected, turning back to watch the shadows reach a flamboyant poinciana tree. One part of her mind estimated that when the tree was engulfed in shade, sunset would be at hand, while the rest of her mind considered Lily's words.

Years ago, when Lily was born, children ran free. They were loved and watched over by all the adults, not just their parents. The only exceptions were the special young ones, usually of the *alii*, the ones being taught to follow in the footsteps of a *kahuna*. Their training was rigorous. The entire history of that particular field was taught in chants. The chosen ones were expected to

learn without aid of books or pencils, simply by listening and repeating. They were being given priceless gifts
and they were taught humility through discipline. In-
struction in chanting included lessons in the proper way
to breathe and the proper time to breathe. All of that,
and more, was taught to the special children.

Liann blinked, fighting back sudden tears. Auntie
knew that she understood. Understood that each of
them had their own destiny to consider, but that somehow they had become entwined. Understood that with
a few words she had placed herself in Liann's young
hands, trusting their strength to guard an extraordinary history and a doubtful future. Liann glanced at the
poinciana tree; half was in sunshine, half in shade. She
turned and walked back into the room, coming to a halt
near Lily.

The old woman looked up, examining Liann's troubled expression. She touched her hand and pointed to
the chair across from her. "Your eyes hold new knowledge," she said calmly. "And some fear. Sit. We must
add to one and dispel the other."

The two women spoke softly until the shade almost
covered the poinciana tree.

Lily glanced outside with serene eyes. "Come," she
said, "it is time." She rose, every inch a queen, and
without looking to see if Liann was following, walked
out to the *lanai*.

*From its soaring ascent in a dark and quiet world to
its descent in silent majesty, the flight of the golden bird
is constant.*

Quietly taking a seat, Liann watched Lily come to a
halt at the deck railing. Turning to face an exact point
on the horizon, the old woman closed her eyes and took

a deep breath. The sun slowly dipped toward the water, surrounding itself with glorious shades of brilliance, commanding the mortals below to pay homage to its beauty.

Sharing its mana with all, kingly in power and grace, the golden bird has no rival.

The unequalled radiance of the evening sun bestowed warmth and energy on every living thing. Lily reached out to the powerful spirit, chanting softly.

Liann's heart raced and she knew if she lived to be a hundred, she would never forget this moment. Lily recited the story of that journey so long ago, recalling the fear, the uncertainty, the prayers for guidance. She told of the bird who guided the courageous people into uncertain waters, then returned to lead them into the valley of their heart.

And goose bumps broke out on Liann's arms when, for the first time, she heard the rest of the story. It was much as she had begun to visualize it: the *'io* was the old woman's personal *aumakua*, or family god, and the sun symbolized the guiding force, the bird who had led those people home.

Bestowing constant benediction, the keeper of the golden bird is graced beyond measure.

The old woman sang in a clear voice that carried softly through the growing darkness. When she stopped her hymn of praise, it was with a promise to greet the golden bird before dawn. And when she turned to Liann, her expression was one of fulfillment.

The two women walked into the house and Lily reached down to turn on a lamp. "You better go now, yeh?"

Liann blinked, both at the glare of light and the woman who stood before her. In those few moments, the transition was complete. Auntie waited for her answer. Also, without further words, she informed Liann that the talking was over. They each had things to do, and no more discussion was necessary.

"I think maybe Cody Hunter be real worried about you, yeh?"

Thrust abruptly into the real world, Liann looked at her watch and groaned. Cody should have been at her house more than half an hour ago. She threw her arms around Lily and hugged her swiftly.

"Don't worry," she said, unwrapping her arms from around the solid woman. "I'll think of something. And, Auntie, please, no more…" She paused, trying to think of a polite way to put it.

"Shenanigans," she said, solving Liann's problem. "I promise. From now on, I stick to my pictures."

"Good." Sudden laughter lit their eyes. Just as quickly it disappeared.

"Aloha, Auntie."

"Aloha, my daughter."

The ride down the bumpy road at night was not something that Liann wanted to repeat in a hurry. It was a real lesson in patience, she decided the third time she tried to speed up and hit a bone-rattling rut. Slowing the car down to a crawl, she wished for just one streetlight on the road. Since that was clearly wasted effort, she tried to think of something cheery to help her calm down, an old trick her mother had taught her that never failed. About the only one she could think of was the fact that she was in her car and not Cody's.

Cody. Good heavens, what was she going to do about him? She glanced quickly at the dashboard clock and groaned aloud. Forty-five minutes late. At least that. Well, there wasn't much she could do about it, she reflected philosophically. Her time would be better spent figuring a way to explain this whole thing to him, because once they put her apology behind them, that would be the next item on the agenda.

He wasn't going to be thrilled to hear that Lily was behind the goings-on at the site. Edging over to the side of the road to avoid a deep rut, she wondered just how much she could expect of the man. She had already tossed the book at him, given him a crash course in understanding the real Hawaii. The fact that he was still hanging around was a testament to something—either his fortitude or her teaching ability. At the moment, she wasn't sure which.

All she had to do, she reminded herself bracingly, was tell him that Lily wasn't being a nuisance just to be a nuisance. Behind all the trivial—no, scratch trivial. Behind all the incidents was a perfectly good reason. At least, Lily thought so. She had tried her brand of reasoning and that hadn't worked. She had tried teaching him her picture method, but she was too impatient to see if that worked. So obviously, she had decided, she had to take things into her own hands.

If I were Cody, Liann wondered pensively, would I buy that? Not hardly. Deciding to come back to that part, she forged ahead—and stopped as if she had run into a brick wall. All she had to do next was convince Cody that Lily really did need her clear view of the horizon, that something *would* have to be done to make the domed roof lower.

Swinging onto the smooth, blacktopped highway, she thought morosely about the upcoming discussion. As far as she could see, there weren't any bright spots. Not a thing she could look forward to. By the time she pulled into her parking area, she still hadn't found a ray of light. She parked next to Cody's BMW and sprinted down the walk.

Slightly surprised to find that he wasn't leaning against the door, she opened it and stepped inside.

"Where the hell have you been?" His voice cut through the dark, then she heard a click and light filled the room.

"Cody! You scared the life out of me. How'd you get in here?"

"The manager," he snapped. "God knows she's seen me around here enough, so when I told her I was worried about you, she opened the door." Brushing that aside, he scowled down at her. "Well?"

"I'm late," she told him, dropping her bag on the chair and trying her best smile.

He ignored it and swore. "I *know* that."

"I mean, I'm sorry I'm late," she amended.

Liann knew she was having trouble concentrating. She even knew why—because she was coping with a startling insight. Once before, when he had come over macho and was pushing a bit too hard, she had thought that she never again wanted to be in the position of reporting her comings and goings to a possessive man. Now, looking at Cody, with his blond hair rumpled from running his hands through it and a worried frown on his face, she knew it made all the difference in the world which man it was and why he was being possessive.

Cody was asking because he was worried, not angry. And he was worried because he cared; his reaction had nothing to do with jealousy. Feeling like the weight of the world had dropped from her shoulders, she closed the door behind her and walked over to him.

Staring down at her lovely smile in bemusement, Cody asked, "Why are you looking at me like that?"

"Because I think I love you."

Chapter Ten

T*hink?* I'll tell you right now, woman, you'd better do a lot more than think about it." Cody reached out and yanked her against him.

"Don't call me woman," she muttered against his throat, her lips still curved up at the corners.

He rested his chin on her head, his arms tightening convulsively. "If you ever do this to me again—"

"Shhh," she interrupted in a soothing whisper. There was tension raging through him. She could feel it in the rapid beat of his heart, in the tremor that ran through his body.

"I've been sitting here in the dark imagining the damnedest things," he said tightly. "Car accidents—"

"I'm a very careful driver," she told him.

"—drowning—"

"I swim like a fish."

"Damn it, Liann! Are you laughing at me?"

She shook her head, touching the tip of her tongue to the pulse racing in his throat in a mute apology.

"You'd better not be," he warned, dropping a quick kiss to the top of her head. "It's not funny."

"You're right, it's not." She nestled closer and said, "I'm really sorry, Cody, and I promise I'll tell you all about it. But do you mind sitting down while we talk?"

He held her away from him and raked her from head to toe with hard gray eyes. "Are you hurt?"

"*No.* There's nothing the matter with me. Honest." She stepped back and held out her hand to him.

Ignoring her gesture, he scooped her up in his arms and strode over to the couch. Still holding her, he sat down at one end and settled her in his lap. "Okay," he said, looking down at her startled face, "talk."

Liann blinked. "Just like that? No leading up to things?"

Now that he had her in his arms and knew she wasn't hurt, Cody took a deep breath and exhaled sharply. He cupped her head with one hand and silently decided that he had gone a bit crazy when she walked through the door.

"Let me start," he said abruptly. "I'm sorry for jumping on you like that. Wherever you've been, whatever you've been doing, you didn't deserve that." He put a finger across her parted lips when she started to interrupt. "You took about ten years off my life tonight and I didn't like the feeling at all. Now," he ended politely, "would you like to tell me where you've been?"

"At Auntie Lily's," she said promptly.

"And you couldn't call?"

Wrinkling her nose at the grim note in his voice, she asked, "Where? You had already left your house, and I certainly didn't expect you to be in here. Besides," she concluded, "Auntie doesn't have a telephone." Sighing, she leaned back, dropping her head in the hollow of his shoulder. "Do you think we could just sit here for a couple of minutes and *not* talk?"

She softened against him, and he nodded. Reaching over to the table beside him, he snagged the telephone and punched out a number. He said tersely, "She's here. Yeah. Just fine," and hung up.

Liann stirred in his arms. "What was all that about?"

"I was worried and called your folks a while ago, trying to track you down." No, he decided, what he had been was panicked. "Anyway, I just wanted to call off the hounds."

Leaning back to look up at him, she said lazily, "Do you always react this way when your date is late?"

"What way?" He absorbed the smile in her warm, brown eyes.

"Practically calling out the National Guard."

"No." And he realized with a jolt that he had passed some invisible barrier, that his life would never be the same. He would never be free of the terror that something might happen to her.

"That's it?" she teased, moving away and leaning back against the padded arm of the couch. "Just 'no'? That's all I get?"

"For now," he told her, feeling his muscles unknot a notch at a time. Eventually, she'd get it all, everything he had, once he got used to the idea himself.

Now that every inch of her wasn't pressed up against him, Cody took a longer look at her. A smile curved her lips, but there was an expression of strain in the clear eyes that mirrored her every emotion, a fragile look about her that he didn't like.

"That last time I talked to you," he began moderately, "you were wearing something you wouldn't dia cuoo, and the only thing you planned to do was read a book." His voice grew more heated. "Would you like to tell me what you've been up to since then?"

"Oh!" She sat up with a jerk. "Cody, I found it!"

"Found what?" he asked blankly.

She threw her arms around his neck and laughed. "The end of the rainbow!"

After nearly throttling him, she settled back against the armrest, sheer bliss animating her features. "You can't believe how exciting it was. I had already finished one book and was in the middle of the second. Never in my life did I dream it would happen that way! I just turned the page, and there it was."

He lifted a strand of hair from her cheek and smoothed it down behind her ear. "There what was?" he asked indulgently. He didn't have the faintest idea what she was talking about. She was happy and that was all that mattered.

She frowned up at him. "The answer!" At his blank look, she added, "the clue. The end of the story!"

"Your legend?" he ventured cautiously.

"Of course, my legend. What else would I be talking about?"

He smiled. "I'm just a little slow tonight, honey. Blame it on delayed reaction." He bent his head and slowly brushed his lips against hers. "Congratulations," he said softly. After a moment's consideration, he asked, "What comes next?"

An anxious look crept into her eyes. "What do you mean?"

Wondering about her sudden tension, he said mildly, "Do you report it to the Institute, write about it for a magazine, or what?"

Her pent-up breath came out in a rush of relief. "Oh, that. Herb lets me handle things pretty much as I want. I'll write it up eventually." Her transparent gaze shifted until she was looking at some middle distance over his shoulder. "There are a few things that have to be straightened up first, though," she said vaguely. "Right now, it's enough that I know."

In a wry voice, he said, "My love, why do I get the feeling that you're leaving out something fairly important?"

In the taut silence that followed, her eyes met his and he flinched at the stark misery in them. She tried to move and his arm tightened around her, holding her where she was. He wanted her where he could feel every emotion flowing through her body. He had a nasty feeling that the other shoe was about to drop, and he wanted every advantage he could get.

"Because I am," she wailed softly. "I don't know how to tell you. Oh, Cody, I'm sorry."

Exasperation and the beginning of real fear sharpened his voice. "For what, for God's sake?"

She flung out her hands. "For everything!" Everything was her fault, she thought miserably. If she hadn't been so persistent about enlarging the cultural department, the plans for the Center wouldn't have been approved. And if they hadn't, Auntie's view wouldn't be threatened. And if it wasn't, she wouldn't be in the position of explaining to Cody—an outsider—that he was the one who had to keep the Center roof out of Auntie's view. And on top of all that, as he was performing that bit of magic, she had to find a way to preserve Auntie's anonymity while adding the proper ending to the legend.

He said carefully, "I think I could handle whatever's coming a little easier if you'd start at the beginning. Your habit of dropping verbal bombs is a bit unnerving. Okay?"

She nodded reluctantly. "Okay." Blinking, she eyed him expectantly.

He shook his head and took a deep breath. It was going to be a long night. "It's your story," he pointed out mildly, then waited with what patience he had for her to collect her thoughts.

"Oh. Well, it all started with the book, of course." Enthusiasm brightened her face. "Cody, you can't imagine the thrill I got when I turned the page and there it was."

"What was?" he asked, narrowing his eyes and deciding that it would be a *very* long night.

"Didn't I tell you?" As soon as she asked, she knew. "Sorry. Listen to this." She quoted the lines about the golden bird and waited expectantly. So did Cody.

"That's it?" he finally asked.

"Of course it is," she said indignantly. "It tells you everything you need to know."

"Oh."

"Don't you see? It isn't a bird that rises in the dark and sets in majesty, it's the sun. The sun spreads its *mana*, is kingly in power and grace and has no rival. The sun is the golden bird. It's symbolic for all the birds, especially the one that led our ancestors to this land. And Auntie is its keeper."

"Well," he said doubtfully, "you're the expert on legends. You should know."

"I do."

There was no doubt in her voice, no tension, so that wasn't the problem. But he didn't like the way she stressed the words "our ancestors," as if she were drawing a line between them. His voice was smooth as steel when he said, "What happened next?"

"Oh. Well, I went up to Auntie's place and...we had a long talk," she finished inadequately. She averted her eyes, but she couldn't stand the silence. When she took a quick peek at his face, she groaned to herself. He had that bulldog look, she decided. He wasn't going to move until she told him everything he wanted to know and every detail was resolved to his satisfaction.

She took a deep breath and plunged in. "I found out that Auntie was behind all of the things happening around here—the men calling in sick, the missing keys, even Mr. Lee's call."

His expression went from stubborn to pure ice. "I thought as much," he said repressively, "but I couldn't prove it. I suppose she thought she had a good reason?"

She nodded. "Yes, but you probably wouldn't agree. If you don't mind, I'll get back to that later. I just wanted it out of the way so I could go on with the rest. Cody, what I'm going to tell you is very personal and confidential. It should never go beyond the two of us."

"Are you sure you want to tell me, honey?" His thumb touched her cheek in a light caress. "It's all right if you don't."

"I have to," she said starkly. "You have to know this before we can go on to...other things." She looked away from the tightening muscle in his jaw, tried concentrating on his chin and realized that wasn't much better. Cody had a very determined chin.

She cleared her throat. "As I said, Auntie is the keeper of the golden bird. Do you have any idea what that means?" Of course he didn't. How could he? He was still working on Saddle Road and Madame Pele. She couldn't expect a man from another world, another culture, to understand a lifetime committed to a legend. Not waiting for his response, she went on.

"It means that when Auntie was an infant, she was selected as the next keeper, the *kahuna*. Her parents handed her over to the current one before she could even walk. She grew up living and breathing the history and legends that told of our people."

She smiled briefly. "Incidentally, I was right about the *'io*. It is her *aumakua*, and she is of royal blood."

"Go on," Cody said grimly, almost as if he were preparing for battle.

"In those days, the training was rigorous. All information was passed down verbally. Chants were chanted to her like nursery rhymes were sung to other children. *Kapus* surrounded her. She couldn't be touched by unclean hands. She had to eat certain foods. For the first ten years of her life, she was kept separate from other children."

She looked up to see if he was listening, and when their eyes met, she had the feeling that he was hearing things she hadn't even said. "Frequently," she continued in a level voice, "she was taken down by the water for more training. Her teacher would stand on one side of the cove and send Auntie to the other side with instructions to chant. Without shouting, she would have to make her chanting heard over the wind and the waves.

"Later, when she learned all she would need to carry on the tradition, she was sent home to wait for the proper time. And when it came, she moved to the house on the hill, because that land always belongs to the keeper of the golden bird."

"Why that particular land?" he asked, knowing he wouldn't like the answer. Tiny tremors were shaking her, and he felt the tension building in every line of her body.

Liann shivered. "Because of the view," she said baldly. "Every day for the rest of her life, her job is to bring up the sun with a chant and chant it to rest at night. To do that, she has to keep it in sight at all times."

He was quick. She'd never had any doubts about that. He put it together with breathtaking speed and laid it out before her.

His voice was matter-of-fact. "You're telling me that once the Center is done, she won't be able to do her job, aren't you?"

Answering his question with another, Liann said, "Do you know what happens to her if she doesn't fulfill the responsibility given her?" Sighing sharply, she closed her eyes and rubbed at the deep furrows of stress between her brows. "Of course you don't. You couldn't." She looked up into bleak gray eyes. "She wanders through eternity, homeless and hungry, unable either to join those who went before her or to take on the form of the *'io*, her *aumakua*."

Cody swore softly. "And you're asking me to do something about it, aren't you?" The strain he felt showed in his voice.

This time when she moved, he didn't try to stop her. She slid from his lap and walked the length of the room in agitation. Turning back, she shook her head and tried to smile. The despair on her face shredded his heart.

"Cody," she answered tenderly, "I couldn't possibly ask you that."

And suddenly she realized that she couldn't. There was nothing he or anyone could do and she wouldn't burden him with guilt over something that wasn't his fault. "What we need is a miracle, and they seem to be in short supply these days." This time, her small smile was ironic. "No, this seems to be a case of the past fighting the future, and the future wins hands down."

And as surely as if she had drawn a line down the center of the room, she placed herself on one side and him on the other.

Cody looked at her, standing as far away from him as she could get and still be in the same room. Her slender, proud body looked fragile in the dim light, but he knew that she had the strength to stand tearless and watch him walk away. Knew, in fact, that she was gearing herself up to do exactly that.

He got to his feet and jammed his hands in his back pockets, sending an intimidating glare across the room at her. Hell, *he* didn't have that kind of strength. He was hurting so much right now, he felt like he'd been beaten with two-by-fours. This delicate woman standing so quietly in her pain was the first he had ever loved, the only one he would ever love. He wanted to put his arms around her and bring back her radiant smile. He not only wanted to find a miracle for her, he wanted to *be* the miracle.

Liann flinched from his look of restrained fury and took another step back. Dear God, why didn't he go? she wondered frantically as she brushed against the wall. Blinking to hold back her tears, she said, "Cody, I—"

He held up his hand to stop her. "No. You've had your say, now it's my turn."

As he crossed the room, everything about him was deliberately intimidating—his stride, his look, his aura of barely controlled violence. He ignored the imaginary line she had drawn and came to a stop right in front of her. In a movement equally as intimidating, he placed a hand on either side of her head, palms to the wall, enclosing her in the warmth of his body.

"Lady," he said roughly, "I have the feeling that you've just been saying goodbye to me." Two tears brimmed over her eyes and trickled down, leaving a silver path on her cheeks. He bent his head and brushed them away with his lips. "I want to promise you a miracle," he said heavily, "but I can't. All I can tell you is that whatever happens, I'm coming back for you!"

His kiss was full of rough hunger, exploding with passion. She moaned and clung to him with desperation, running her hands through his thick, springy hair. Murmuring incoherently, he pressed her to the wall. She was still there, gasping for breath, when the door closed softly behind him.

* * *

"Hal, have you seen Cody today?" Liann asked, trying to ignore the fact that this was the third morning in a row she had asked him the same question.

"Nope," the lanky foreman replied. "But he called and gave me working orders, just like he did yesterday, and the day before."

"Oh." Liann looked around her. The place seemed busier than ever. Lily had kept her promise and all the men were back. Cement was being poured and spread and things appeared to be moving forward with alarming speed. "Is it my imagination," she asked casually, "or are things going at a faster pace than usual?"

"You got a good eye, Liann," he said, squinting across the yard at one of the cement mixers. "Cody had me hire some more workers to make up for the hours we lost when so many of the men were out."

"Oh." So much for miracles, she thought, wandering forlornly back to the trailer and wondering if she would ever see Cody again. It was one thing for a man to make a dramatic statement about coming back, another entirely to actually do it. And God only knew she couldn't blame him. She had tried right from the beginning to show him how different they were. Apparently she had succeeded only too well.

Maybe it was all for the best, she consoled herself, knowing that she was lying through her teeth. Even if he did come back, what would he find? The same troublesome woman he left, one who wasn't easily changed. A woman so tied to the past she sometimes forgot what day of the week it was. A woman who didn't want to leave her family, friends or home. A woman who was attuned to a far less pragmatic world than the one in which he functioned.

About the only thing he might find encouraging was that her old wounds had mostly healed and she was learning to trust again. Not a heck of a lot, she admitted, when it was balanced against all the rest.

Making an abrupt decision, she turned on her heel and headed back to where she had left the foreman.

"Hal," she said, when he broke away from a group of workers, "there's nothing for me to do around here, so I'm going over to work at my folks' place. They're in Kauai for a couple of days and I'm using the computer in their office."

One of the nice things about her job, she reflected twenty minutes later when she opened the office door at her parents' place, was her personal freedom. She might joke about Herb being a Simon Legree, but he actually gave her a pretty free rein. If she said that she was researching something and wouldn't be in, he just told her to leave a number where he could reach her. Right now, she was especially grateful for the latitude he allowed her. She couldn't bear to be in the office where Cody might just drop in to see Herb. She simply wasn't up to an accidental meeting.

And if she stretched things just a bit, she could say she was doing research. This computer was definitely unchartered territory. So far, it had a distressing tendency to chew up things and spit them out in some dark hole where she couldn't retrieve them. Uncovering it, she pulled out the manual and opened it to page one.

"But I'll get you straightened out," she murmured optimistically. "Just give me a couple of minutes."

"I can't wait that long," Cody's deep voice informed her.

Chapter Eleven

Cody!''

She turned around and stared at the man in the doorway, her eyes devouring him. He looked tired, impatient and absolutely magnificent.

"You're dressed up," she blurted out in surprise, taking in the gray slacks, white shirt and yellow tie. Even for a man of Cody's conservative nature, that was going a bit far for a construction site. And in the two months that she had known him, she had never seen him so weary. He looked like he needed to sleep for a week.

She blinked nervously, not liking the way his gray eyes were examining her, feature by feature. She knew she looked awful. Stress always left her looking like a sad, underfed waif.

"God, you're beautiful," he said huskily, spreading his arms. "Come here and let me hold you."

For a moment, Liann forgot all the anxieties that had been haunting her. She flew into his arms, felt them close around her and knew she had come home. Luxuriating in the feel of him, she flung her arms around his neck and slowly traced the smooth, well-defined muscles of his shoulders. His lips covered hers and her fingers tangled in the thickness of his hair, shaping his skull, holding him close.

"I've missed you," she murmured, tilting her head accommodatingly so his lips could touch the vulnerable spot behind her ear. "You've been gone forever."

"Only three days," he muttered, working his way down the tender hollow of her throat. Liann's lips curved in a deeply feminine smile as his arms tightened, denying the practical statement.

"Forever," she repeated when they both drew back for breath.

He looked down, his gray gaze traveling over her face, one thumb gently touching the lavender shadows under her eyes. "You didn't have these when I left."

"I hadn't spent three sleepless nights worrying," she said with stark simplicity, knowing that the time had passed for evasions.

He wrapped his arm around her waist and urged her outside by the pool, murmuring, "Oh, ye of little faith." Leading her to a double lounge chair situated in the shade, he dropped into it and drew her down beside him. "I told you I'd be back."

Liann curled up beside him, resting her head on his shoulder. "Somehow," she retorted, nestling closer to soften the effect, "I've heard more inspiring last words."

Cody reached up and unbuttoned his collar. After loosening his tie, he leaned back, closed his eyes and sighed. "God, it's been a long three days."

"Why were you gone so long?" she asked tentatively, feeling her stomach lurch with anxiety. If he had bad news, she wanted it quickly.

"A miracle takes longer than it used to," he murmured, a faint smile curving his lips.

It took a moment to sink in. When it did, Liann stiffened and slowly sat up, looking down at the picture of male satisfaction. "Cody? Darn you, Cody Hunter, open your eyes and look at me! What do you mean, a miracle?"

Instead of doing as she commanded, he hooked his arm around her and gently pulled her back against him. "Is that any way to talk to a hero?" he complained, running his hand down her back and stopping at the elegant curve of her bottom.

"You're driving me crazy," she told him.

He opened one interested eye.

"Not that way," she said, lying through her teeth. "Sit up and talk to me."

"You're a hard woman."

"You don't know the half of it," she assured him serenely, smiling at his look of contentment and, for the first time in three days, allowing herself to hope that there could be a happy ending for everyone involved. "Talk to me, Cody Hunter."

He pushed himself higher on the lounge and turned to face her. "I could have avoided a lot of heartache for all of us, if I had just used my head," he said in a voice filled with disgust. "Our problem was that we were all focused on the roof of the Center, and there wasn't a damn thing I could do about that."

Liann frowned. "I don't understand."

"There are two buildings involved in the problem, honey," he said with a sudden grin. "Think about it for a minute."

She looked at him, prisms of gold lighting the brown of her eyes. "You mean—"

"Yep," he said complacently. "I'm putting a second story on Lily's place."

"It's so simple," she said, stunned. "Why on earth didn't any of us think about it sooner?"

"Because we all saw the Center as the problem. And Lily was no help at all when she kept harping about her pictures. She kept telling us to concentrate on the domed roof."

"So tell me everything you've been doing," Liann ordered.

"I had Herb call an emergency meeting of the planning committee and gave them a heartrending story about the roof ruining the view of one of our most eminent citizens. I told them you had assured me that it was rotten public relations, and if she was willing to go through the inconvenience of having her place remodeled, they should be willing to pay for it."

"Did they go for it?" she asked, looking at him in awe.

"Yeah." He grinned again. "I didn't know how many of Lily's old cronies were on the committee. No problem at all."

"Then what?" she prompted.

"Then I had to sell Lily on the project."

"Oh, dear."

"That," he said wryly, "is putting it mildly. You can't believe the arguments she had. She didn't want men working up there, she didn't want the noise, she didn't want her birds disturbed, *she* didn't want to be disturbed, she didn't—''

''I get the idea. Who won?''

''I did. I had to,'' he said simply. ''There was no other answer.''

''And I suppose she realized it.''

''Eventually. I told her the birds would get accustomed to the noise.''

''And she agreed?''

He took in a deep breath of exasperation as he remembered. ''Eventually. About that and everything else. But she's one tough lady and she didn't make it easy. She switched roles so many times, I never knew who I was dealing with. If the Institute ever needs a hard-nosed negotiator, they ought to call on her.''

Liann grinned, wishing that she had been there.

''I spent the whole day up there, hammering out conditions and doing a quick survey, just to make sure the whole thing was feasible.''

''Conditions?'' Liann asked.

''Mmmm. We'll have a double crew up there so we can get it done as quickly as possible. We're to be aware of her birds at all times and make as little noise as possible. No one is to be there before dawn, and everyone leaves well before sunset. Apparently,'' he said blandly, ''she goes to bed early.''

He reached out and ruffled her silky brown hair, unutterably touched by her transparent happiness. She *cared* so much, he thought with a fierce surge of love. ''Well, honey,'' he murmured, ''have we settled all of Lily's problems?''

She nodded, ''I think so. I'm sure she'll let us know if we've forgotten anything.''

He reached out for her hand, lacing their fingers together so their hands were palm to palm. "Then, can we concentrate on us for a while?"

"Cody, before you say anything, there are a couple of things I have to tell you."

He felt the nervous tremor in her fingers and laid her hand against his thigh, holding it in place with the weight of his. He was getting too old for this constant ebb and flow of adrenaline, he decided wearily, wondering what problems she had conjured up in his absence. It was too damned exhausting. "Okay," he said evenly, "you go first."

"While you were gone," she began hesitantly, faintly alarmed by the growing grimness in his eyes, "I had a lot of time to think. I said things that night at my place that weren't fair to you."

His surprise was obvious. "Like what?"

"When I was telling you about Lily, I said you wouldn't understand. I meant that you couldn't because you weren't born here."

"You were probably right," he muttered.

She shook her head impatiently. "You may never sympathize with or believe in our cultural . . . oddities, but that isn't important. I don't know why you're looking so surprised," she said testily. "I'm simply trying to explain something. When I was telling you about Lily's training, I might as well have been talking about an alien land. I could see you just sitting there shaking your head over the whole thing."

She reached out and touched his cheek with a slim finger. "But you understood the most important thing. Whether or not you believed in what she was doing, you recognized her dedication and commitment. And that's what you responded to."

With an effort that was obvious to the man sitting so quietly at her side, she raised her lashes and looked straight into his eyes. "You're a man of honor and integrity," she said quietly, "and that's far more important than the place of your birth."

Her fingers slid from his cheek to cover his parted lips. "No—" she smiled wryly "—this isn't easy, so let me finish while I'm on a roll. The other thing has to do with us."

Cody reached up and captured the small hand by his face, his fingers locking gently around her wrist. She was so delicate, yet she had the strength of a warrior within her. He could toss her over one shoulder and never feel her weight, yet she had the power to break him in half. He didn't know where she was heading, but damned if he was going to sit still while she tried to walk away from him again.

"If you think for one minute," he said tightly, "that I'm listening to another farewell speech, you're out of your mind."

She blinked, thrown off course by his interruption. "That's not what—"

"I've spent three hellish days away from you."

"Mine weren't so easy, you know."

Ignoring her muttered comment, he said, "I took care of every problem you threw at me the other night. There isn't a thing I overlooked."

"Knowing your penchant for details," she murmured with a tiny smile, "I'm sure you're right."

"I wrecked more peoples' schedules, interrupted more meetings . . . what did you say?"

"I said I'm sure you're right," she repeated serenely.

"Oh." He shook her hand lightly, demanding her full attention. "What I'm telling you, my love," he said aggressively, "is that in spite of whatever differences you think we have, we belong together—"

"That's exactly what I was trying to say."

"—and that *nothing* is going to keep us from getting married!" He stopped, examining her politely attentive expression. "You were?"

She nodded, laughing at him with her eyes.

Exhaling sharply, he shook his head like a punch-drunk fighter. "The floor's yours, love."

Tugging her hands loose, she raised them to his face, tracing in loving detail the stubborn angle of his jaw, the lines fanning out from the corners of his eyes. "When you walked out the other night, I knew that I would be crippled for life if you didn't come back," she said with a direct honesty that stunned him.

"I knew that whatever had happened to me in the past, everything would be different with you. I knew that when you came back, I would have only one thing to say."

Not moving a muscle, afraid to stop the gentle flow of her voice, Cody waited, knowing with instinctive certainty that he had won.

"I will marry you, Cody Hunter." The soft formality of her voice, the flow of her words, so different from her usual speech pattern, was incredibly touching. "I will go where you go, continue my work wherever we are, love you for all time and know that I am loved in the same way." She wrapped her arms around his neck and moved her lips against his throat. "Will you have me, Cody Hunter?"

His arms tightened around her convulsively, pulling her closer, holding the soft woman who carried within her the strength of all women. "Will I have you? Dear God, Liann, you tear my heart out. I love you," he pledged solemnly, knowing what it had cost her to even consider leaving the land that bound her so closely and spiritually. "I'll always love you, and I'll always take care of you."

Much later, he leaned back and looked down at her love-softened face. "I didn't even have to bribe you," he teased lazily.

She blinked up at him, an interested gleam in her eyes. "With what?"

"Some property that's for sale down by the lagoon."

Cautious excitement warred with the interest. "What would I do with it?"

"Share it with me," he said promptly. "Build a house, raise kids, raise hell, whatever you want to do as long as you do it with me."

"Do you mean it?" she whispered, a smile curving her lips and spreading to her bright eyes.

"Honey, you'll never know what your offer meant to me," he said roughly. "I'll cherish it as long as I live. But I can't take you away from here. This is where you belong. I've already talked to Terry about moving my office to Kona permanently. What do you say?"

She brought his head down to hers and kissed him. "Exactly what I said before. Cody Hunter, I love you."

The wedding of Liann Murphy and Cody Hunter was the second big event in the month of October, following the opening of the new Center. The reception took place at the home of the bride's parents.

Liann Murphy Hunter took a sip of champagne and looked through the crowd of well-wishers for her husband, finally spotting him talking to Mr. Lee.

"Well," Megan asked her glowing sister, "is my new brother going to survive living in 'haunted' Hawaii?"

"You're the self-designated prophet around here," Liann said, smiling, "you tell me."

"He will. He'll never stop trying to find explanations, but he'll make it."

Liann laughed, a spontaneous lilting sound that had the people nearby smiling. "That reminds me of the latest episode at the Center."

"What happened?"

"Cody was helping me set up the displays before the opening. Each morning we'd come in and find things moved around. So Cody called Sammy, who'd been hired as the night watchman, and asked him about it."

"And Sammy told him straight that he hadn't touched a thing?"

"Right. Then Cody swore that Lily was having one last bit of fun with us. When we asked her, she denied it."

"So?" Megan asked, as if she already knew what was coming.

Liann shrugged. "We had the Center blessed, and everything stayed right where it belonged."

"But Cody's still looking for other, more logical, explanations?"

"Of course." She saw her husband working his way through the crowd, heading toward her with a deter-

mined gleam in his eye. She smiled and said absently,
"When he doesn't have other things on his mind."

A heavy hand on Cody's shoulder stopped him in his
tracks.

"What did I tell you, Cody Hunter?" Lily beamed at
him. "I got my picture, you got yours!"

Pictures were the last thing on Cody's mind several
hours later. He stepped out of the shower and pulled a
large towel off the rack. He dried himself hastily, then
went to the bedroom door and came to a sudden halt,
stunned recognition in his eyes as he watched Liann.

She stood facing him across the length of the large
room. The large bed, its sheet and blanket pulled to the
bottom, was softly illuminated by a small lamp. Sheer
curtains undulated the breeze drifting through the open
sliding glass doors.

She had on a silky white thing that lovingly hugged
her body, its lower edge flirting around her ankles. With
a small, welcoming smile, she fingered a slim strap, and
in tantalizing degrees, the cloth slid from her shoulders
to rest on her small, high breasts. It clung to her beaded
nipples for endless moments before dropping, catching
and draping around the sweet flare of her hips. Finally,
it slid one last time, pooling around her bare feet, and
she opened her arms to him in an ageless gesture of
feminine welcome.

Liann felt no surprise when she turned and saw Cody
draped in a towel knotted loosely at his waist. He leaned
in the doorway, watching every move she made, every
breath she took. The waiting was over, his eyes prom-

ised. He padded softly across the thick carpeting and took her into his arms.

Much later, when Cody reached out in the middle of the night and drew her closer, his hand settling possessively on one bare breast, Liann smiled.

Pictures were all right, she reflected, snuggling back against the warmth of her husband, but not nearly as interesting as the real thing!

*   *   *   *   *

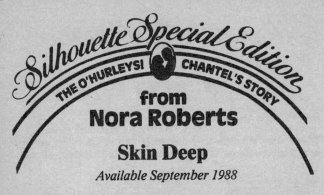

Silhouette Special Edition

THE O'HURLEYS! — CHANTEL'S STORY

from
Nora Roberts

Skin Deep

Available September 1988

The third in an exciting new series about the lives and
loves of triplet sisters—

In May's *The Last Honest Woman* (SE #451), Abby
finally met a man she could trust ... then tried to
deceive him to protect her sons.

In July's *Dance to the Piper* (SE #463), it took some
very fancy footwork to get reserved recording mogul
Reed Valentine dancing to effervescent Maddy's
tune....

In *Skin Deep* (SE #475), find out what kind of heat it
takes to melt the glamorous Chantel's icy heart.
Available in September.

COMING NEXT MONTH

#604 TYLER—Diana Palmer
Most men frightened shy Nell Regan, but her new ranch foreman,
Tyler Jacobs, was different. Could his gentle strength unlock her
heart's secret passion? LONG, TALL, TEXANS TRILOGY—Book
Three!

#605 GOOD VIBRATIONS—Curtiss Ann Matlock
Stumbling on her treadmill of stress and tension, uptight Jillian
Aldritt met happy-go-lucky beach boy Max Jensen. And in Max's
arms, she tasted a freedom she'd never dreamed of....

#606 O'DANIEL'S PRIDE—Susan Haynesworth
Feisty Lera O'Daniel was struggling to save her family's farm. Times
were hard... until dashing Miles Macklin came along. Could he be
the answer to Lera's prayers?

#607 THE LOVE BANDIT—Beverly Terry
When reporter Hester Arlen interviewed the infamous Love Bandit,
she didn't expect to fall for his charms. Could a man who broke so
many hearts give his to Hester?

#608 TRUE BLISS—Barbara Turner
Trade negotiator Matthew Morgan thought big business held the
ultimate high-stakes excitement—until dazzling Bliss Kellaway blazed
into his life and showed him love had the highest stakes of all.

#609 COME BE MY LOVE—Annette Broadrick
When lawyer Gregory Duncan escaped to his friend's secluded chalet
for a much-needed rest, he didn't bargain on meeting Brandi Martin,
an irresistible woman—who desperately needed his help....

AVAILABLE THIS MONTH:

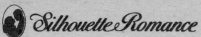

Silhouette Romance

LONG, TALL TEXANS

A Trilogy by Diana Palmer

Bestselling Diana Palmer has rustled up three rugged heroes in a trilogy sure to lasso your heart! The titles of the books are your introduction to these unforgettable men:

CALHOUN

In June, you met Calhoun Ballenger. He wanted to protect Abby Clark from the world, but could he protect her from himself?

JUSTIN

Calhoun's brother, Justin—the strong, silent type—had a second chance with the woman of his dreams, Shelby Jacobs, in August.

TYLER

October's long, tall Texan is Shelby's virile brother, Tyler, who teaches shy Nell Regan to trust her instincts—especially when they lead her into his arms!

Don't miss TYLER, the last of three gripping stories from Silhouette Romance!

If you missed any of Diana Palmer's Long, Tall Texans, order them by sending your name, address and zip or postal code, along with a check or money order for $1.95 for each book ordered, plus 75¢ postage and handling, payable to Silhouette Reader Service to:

In Canada	In U.S.A.
P.O. Box 609	901 Fuhrmann Blvd.
Fort Erie, Ontario	P.O. Box 1396
L2A 5X3	Buffalo, NY 14269-1396

Please specify book title with your order.

SRLTT-R